# Brothers

## SUSAN RIZZO

Saint Petersburg, Florida

Copyright © 2020 Susan Rizzo

Print ISBN: 978-1-64718-884-9
Epub ISBN: 978-1-64718-885-6
Mobi ISBN: 978-1-64718-886-3

All rights reserved. No part of this publication may be reproduced, stored in a retrieval system, or transmitted in any form or by any means, electronic, mechanical, recording or otherwise, without the prior written permission of the author.

Published by BookLocker.com, Inc., St. Petersburg, Florida.

Printed on acid-free paper.

This is a work of historical fiction, based on actual persons and events. The author has taken creative liberty with many details to enhance the reader's experience.

BookLocker.com, Inc.
2020

First Edition

## Parents' & Teachers' Guide

As a teacher for 20 years, I know the importance of teaching students higher order thinking skills, such as inferencing, deductive reasoning, point of view, foreshadowing, summarizing, predicting, character analysis, comparing and contrasting, forming an opinion, and being able to support conclusions with evidence from the text. It is equally important to help students develop a rich vocabulary.

Brothers was written with all of this in mind. It was originally created to be used in a classroom setting to teach both reading comprehension and about the Holocaust. However, in these uncertain times in which we now find ourselves, it can just as easily be used by parents who are homeschooling their children.

Brothers is historical fiction and has rich vocabulary. It can be used for a Book Club, small group instruction, as a read aloud, or for independent reading.

I have also created a comprehensive guide to support all hard-working teachers and parents who are trying to improve their child's reading comprehension. In the guide you will find vocabulary and discussion questions for each chapter using the strategies mentioned above. Finally, I have provided ideas and examples of final projects that can be assigned. At your discretion you can choose which parts of it you'd like to use, or use it all.

With the help of this guide, parents will be able to work with their children at home, as it will "guide" you through the chapters with appropriate higher order thinking questions.

To order a copy of this 30 page guide, complete with graphic organizers, please email me at brothersbysusan@hotmail.com. The cost for each guide is $10.00 and due to copyright infringement laws cannot be copied. Once you've placed your request, I will provide payment options. After receiving payment, a copy of this guide will be emailed to you.

If you have questions about using this guide once you've received it, you can email me at the address above or visit my website: brothersbysusan.com.

<u>Brothers</u> covers many themes, including:

- The Power of One
- Brotherhood
- Bullying
- The Importance of Reading
- How Personality and Temperament Form Opinions
- Standing Up For What You Believe In
- The Importance of Different Abilities
- The Power of Propaganda/Advertising
- Opposing Ideologies
- True Courage

I truly hope you enjoy reading my story as much as I have enjoyed writing it.

# German Translations

ach du grofser Gott – oh great God or dear God, used when in distress
ach du lieber Gott – Dear God! An expression of surprise
achtung – pay attention, be on guard
bleib – stay
braver hund – good dog!
brummen – growl
Deutsch – German
donauwelle – German cake made with cherries & topped with buttercream & chocolate
fass – attack
Frau – Mrs.
fuss - heel
Gott – God
Herr – Mr.
Herzlichen Gluckwunsch zum Geburtstag – Happy Birthday!
kind – kid (pronounced with a short "i")
kinder – kids (pronounced with a short "i"), children
kuchen – cake
mama – mom
mieze – an insult, as in calling Hans a little girl
mutter – mother
muttering – mothering
Obergruppenfuhrers – one of the Third Reich's paramilitary ranks; one of Hitler's senior leaders

ogottogottogott – oh my God, oh my God, oh my God – used
when in distress
oh mein Gott – oh my God
papa – dad
platz – lie down
setzen – sit
suche – search
vater – father

## -1-

Danny gripped the railing with both hands. He leaned into the wind and squinted over the choppy waves. He couldn't believe they were finally on their way. Far in the distance, he thought he could see a giant figure rising against the sky. The ship rolled slightly and the ever-present pressure at his hip became more pronounced. Automatically, Danny's hand slid down and comforted his constant companion.

"Don't worry, Fritz," he soothed the huge German Shepherd at his side. "We're almost there."

As he turned back to the railing he smiled at the fact that his dog had never shown fear in combat, but was frightened by the gentle rolling of the ship. Reflecting on the past several eventful years, Danny thought about how Fritz had been with him since the beginning of what had turned into the adventure of a lifetime. He thought back to that summer day in 1937. No one could have imagined what was about to transpire.

\*\*\*\*\*\*\*\*\*\*\*\*\*\*\*\*\*\*\*\*\*\*\*\*\*\*\*\*\*\*\*\*\*\*\*\*

Emma Wolf left the skillet heating on the stove and went to get the eggs and sausage. She paused at the window to admire her tiny garden next to their dilapidated shed. Jacob said it couldn't be repaired and he was going to tear it down one day, but he'd been saying that for years. The warm June sun streamed into the kitchen mitigated by a cool morning breeze. The combination lifted both her spirits and a tendril of her light blond hair that had drifted across her cheek.

Absently she tucked the errant strand back behind her ear and dumped the sausages into the pan. As she turned to go wake her boys they surprised her, bursting through the door engrossed in hurried whispers. Seeing her, they fell silent and slipped into their chairs at the table. Emma turned back to the stove with a smile and a sigh. She knew what was coming. All the signs were there. Hans, normally disheveled and sleepy, sat alert and neatly dressed. She could feel his startlingly beautiful eyes on her back and could hear his younger brother, Danny, whispering, urging him on. She steeled her resolve and turned to them with steaming plates of food.

"Guess what," Hans began tentatively, "Herr Schmidt's dog, Daisy, had a litter! There are five puppies and he said he can't keep them all. So he's giving them away!"

Here he paused, letting that sink in while his brother squirmed beside him, willing him to say what they had rehearsed before coming down to breakfast.

"Pleeease, Mama! My birthday is coming up in a few weeks..."

Hans was going to be celebrating his 16$^{th}$ birthday and this was a big year for a young German boy. Boys of that age generally got a special gift commemorating their passage into "adulthood."

Hans continued since his mama hadn't stopped him yet, "I promise I'll take care of the puppy. I'll walk and feed him, and clean up after him every day."

When his mutter put her hands on her hips, Hans knew it was a sign that she was losing patience and was about to say, "No." So he quickly got in the last few words of his plea.

"Have you considered that having my own dog will help teach me responsibility, which you keep telling me I lack….Please, Mama," Hans implored. Danny had come up with that last part about learning responsibility and Hans figured it was worth a try.

Danny was silently rooting for his brother, as he, too, wanted a dog more than anything else.

Emma looked into Hans' eyes and they almost melted her. His eyes were extraordinary – they were blue like most Germans, but they had an unusual tiny circle of green within the blue that gave him a unique, beguiling look. However, she was exhausted from this daily tirade of begging from her older son.

It was the summer of 1937. The Wolf family lived in a small home in the poorest part of Guben, Germany, close to the border of Poland. It was a mixed community. While predominantly German, there were many Polish families, as well as a small sprinkling of Jewish families residing there as well. Most of the Jewish families they knew lived in the more affluent section of Gorlitz, a town bordering their own.

Guben was located on the Lusatian Neisse River in the state of Brandenburg, Germany. The land surrounding the town of approximately 50,000 people was covered by pine forests and lakes. Most importantly, it was still a time of peace and friendship among the different nationalities.

While the houses were almost literally on top of each other, the Wolfs at least had a small yard surrounding their property, which was a luxury in that poor area. The town always seemed to be covered in a thin layer of grit from the weapons factories the Nazis had set up. The pretty buckets of perennials on most doorsteps did little to liven up the neighborhood. Though it was a dreary residential area, fortunately it was a tight-knit community where neighbors looked after each other and each other's kinder. It was rare that any kind got away with any mischief without someone seeing and reporting it to the appropriate parent.

"Hans, we've been over this a thousand times," Frau Wolf responded, "I know how badly you want a dog and I truly wish you could have one. But a dog has to eat and you know we can barely feed ourselves. And if you think you're wearing me down, you're not, you're just wearing me out. Now, eat your breakfast."

Emma got up and began to clean the skillet. Behind her, the boys ate silently, their sullen moods readily apparent.

"What are you boys doing today?" Emma inquired trying to lighten the atmosphere, which had suddenly turned gloomy.

Danny pushed his shaggy, sandy colored hair out of his eyes and answered, "We're picking up Chaim and heading to the park." While Hans resembled their papa with his dark brown hair and slight frame, Danny definitely looked more like his mutter. He was by no means fat...that could never have happened with their meager meals. But, he was soft around the middle since he didn't get the exercise his brother got by playing sports almost daily. He had his mutter's light blue eyes and her gentle disposition. He was much more easy-going, considerate, and thoughtful than his brother.

"Good. When you stop at Chaim's, please bring this casserole to Frau Schwartz. You know she hasn't been feeling well and we need to help out."

As she stopped by the table to pick up their dirty dishes she put her arm around Hans' shoulder in a small act of comfort, and again was shocked at how tall her boy had grown. Soon, she knew, he would be a man.

While Hans wondered why they needed to help Chaim's family; who had more money than Gott, according to Hans' papa, Jacob; he knew better than to say anything. Chaim's family was more than generous to the Wolfs. In fact, the only time Hans wasn't hungry was when he ate dinner at their house, which was usually about three times a week. The food there was always plentiful and Frau Schwartz just laughed when he'd ask for seconds, something he could never do at home. She'd tease him about having a hollow leg, as no matter how much he ate he never seemed to gain an ounce.

Chaim's papa, Herr Schwartz, owned and ran the local grocery store located in the downtown area where there were a variety of other businesses and the town's only bank. It was a prosperous business, though it could not in any way account for their wealth. Hans had heard his mutter say, during one of his frequent eavesdropping sessions, that Frau Schwartz's vater had been a rich banker and being the only child, she had inherited everything upon her parents' deaths. Whenever Hans and Danny were sent to do the shopping, Herr Schwartz would always give them extra. If they ordered four sausages, they inevitably came home with six. When they bought cheese, flour, sugar, or rice there was always more in the package than they had paid for. Nothing was ever said, but in gratitude, Frau Wolf would do all their mending. She was an accomplished seamstress, and it was her way of giving back for all their kindness and generosity. Frau Wolf would also sew pretty doilies and lace runners for Chaim's mutter, who would "ooh" and "ahh" over them like they were prize possessions. The two families had been friends for many years since Hans and Chaim started to play together when they were eight years old. Chaim was only a month older than Hans.

Frau Schwartz was aware that Hans looked after Chaim. While her son was on the chubby side and large for his age, he was a gentle soul. When other boys would cruelly make fun of his weight, Hans always had his back. While Hans was certainly lacking in many areas, loyalty wasn't one of them.

Anyway, thought Emma, fortunately that ended this latest session of Hans' beseeching her to get a dog. Since Hans and Danny would be out playing ball with their friends for the rest of the day, she felt relieved at having the rest of the afternoon free from listening to Hans' pleading. She had enough to keep her busy, that was for sure. She was a housewife, a mutter, and a part time seamstress for her neighbors. It seemed as if there were never enough hours in the day to get her chores done. Since her husband lost his job as a cobbler when the government forced his business to close in 1936, the only work he could get to support his family was downtown in one of the Nazi weapons factories. Being a gentle, peaceful man, he hated every minute of it. Jacob worked long hours and still barely earned enough to house and feed their growing boys. Secretly it broke her heart not to be able to get Hans a dog. Even though she herself loved animals, her husband stood firm on the matter. They just couldn't afford it and that was that.

## -2-

As Emma went through her day doing her chores, she hummed off-key to herself and thought about how fortunate she really was. She had a loving husband, who would do anything for their family, and two healthy young boys. Granted they fought constantly, but she knew, without a doubt, that they loved each other deeply. However, their small family was not without their share of difficulties and tribulations. Money, or rather lack thereof, was always one of those difficulties. More traumatic to their family was that Danny, who had just turned twelve, had been born with a club foot. Fortunately it wasn't a painful foot abnormality. However, it caused him to walk with an awkward gait. It prevented him from playing sports like the rest of the boys in the neighborhood. It also subjected him to a lot of teasing from his peers. On top of that disability, Danny was also afflicted with extreme near-sightedness. Emma was aware that both of these disabilities could be corrected if they weren't so poor, and though Danny never complained, both she and Jacob felt guilty that he had to suffer with them. Nevertheless, he was a very bright, determined boy who always sought and found other activities to keep himself busy and happy. Danny also knew that when the bullying got to be too much, all he needed to do was let Hans know. While scrawny and small for his age, Hans had the heart of a lion, and very few kinder ever messed with him.

Even though Danny couldn't participate in most of the games his brother played, Hans was his idol. When he wasn't fighting with him about inconsequential matters, he followed Hans wherever he could. Hans and the neighborhood kinder had taken to playing baseball fairly frequently. The sport had been introduced a year ago, in 1936, and seemed to have gained in popularity almost overnight. While Danny's club foot kept him from running, he'd make himself useful by retrieving errant balls and cheering on Hans' team.

As usual, on their way to Mayer Park, they stopped to pick Chaim up. Since Chaim came from a wealthy Jewish family, he always had the latest toys which he willingly shared with his friends. He lived in the more prosperous community of Gorlitz that bordered theirs. His home was at least twice the size of theirs and Chaim even had his own room, which was the envy of all the boys in their neighborhood. As they climbed the steps to his wrap around porch, the boys couldn't believe their ears. Was that a puppy bark they heard???

They rushed the rest of the way to the door and sure enough, there in the foyer was a beautiful purebred German Shepherd puppy jumping on their friend. They had long ago learned that they never needed to knock to enter the Schwartz's household. They had always been welcomed and treated like family. So when the pup spotted the boys entering the foyer, he just about bowled them over in his exuberance for more attention and new friends.

"Ach du lieber Gott!" yelled Hans as he rolled on the floor with the puppy, "When did you get him?! How old is he? What's his name?"

Chaim laughed and told him, "My family celebrated my birthday last night. He is four months old and I named him Fritz. Isn't he amazing?" Then he added, "And Fritz isn't even the best part!"

"What could be better than a puppy?" exclaimed Hans as he continued to play with the pup. He was the most adorable thing Hans had ever seen and what he wished for more than anything else in the world. He was bewildered that Chaim could think that there was something else that could be better.

Even so, that "something else" proved to be pretty cool. Chaim's parents had also bought him an air rifle. Both Hans and Danny itched to try it out and Chaim promised they could shoot it with him the next day.

To Hans' delight, Chaim slipped a leash on Fritz and brought him along with them to the park. When they arrived, Luca, Noah, Henry, and Frank were already there tossing the ball around and arguing, as usual, about who was the best fielder. Chaim handed the leash to Danny to take care of Fritz while he and Hans raced off to join their friends. Danny couldn't believe his good fortune, and for the first time ever he was thrilled that he couldn't play the stupid game. And for the first time ever, Hans was jealous of his little brother.

Hans was very athletic and a natural born leader. It was an unspoken rule that he would always be the captain of one of the teams. Yet, today Hans wasn't playing up to par. He kept watching Danny and Fritz and was wishing he was the one playing with Chaim's puppy.

Danny had the time of his life with Fritz as they rough housed and Fritz chased sticks with boundless energy. When it started to get dark and they headed home, Danny's happiness continued as Chaim let Danny hold the leash and walk Fritz home. Chaim had always been his favorite of Hans' friends. He never teased him or made fun of him, as most of the other boys did from time to time, especially Henry. Danny assumed Chaim was just being nice to him because he couldn't play ball with them. Yet he still found it strange…if Fritz was his own dog, he didn't think he would have been so generous.

Not surprisingly when the Wolf boys got home they couldn't stop talking about Chaim's new dog.

"You're not going to believe it!" Hans excitedly told his parents. "Chaim's parents got him a German Shepherd puppy! He is the cutest thing I've ever seen! Danny got to play with him all afternoon while I was playing baseball. He also got to walk Fritz home." Looking Danny in the eye, he continued, "Seeing as he got to play with him, I would have thought he should have let me walk him home though. Don't you agree?" Hans' disappointment led him to complain about Danny. He had great difficulty dealing with his emotions, and his impulsivity often got him in trouble.

Desperately trying to change the subject before the boys started to argue, and her husband lost his patience, Emma quickly replied, "Well yes, I think that would have been a fair thing to do. I'm sure Danny just didn't think of it. And how is Frau Schwartz feeling?"

As expected, that shut the boys up pretty quickly. In all the excitement, they had forgotten to ask. They had left the casserole sitting on an end table in the foyer, so lost were they in their enthusiasm over Fritz. They had been brought up to have good manners, and looked sheepishly at each other when they realized they had been rude, which was a big taboo in their home.

"We're really sorry," Danny responded to the silent, gentle criticism. "We didn't even see her. Right after we met Fritz, Chaim put a leash on him and we left for the park."

Their parents looked at them with disappointment, but also with understanding. The boys asked if they could go over to Chaim's the next day to shoot his air rifle, and they promised to be more polite and to even offer to help Frau Schwartz with her chores. At this, Emma and Jacob acquiesced, but not without several warnings about being careful and not pointing the gun at each other.

"You can take an eye out with that thing," cautioned their mutter several times. Little did she know at the time that her words were prophetic.

## -3-

The boys couldn't get dressed fast enough the next day. They did their chores without protest and when finally allowed to leave, raced each other to Chaim's house. Well, perhaps raced wasn't accurate...Hans jogged at what he considered to be an excruciatingly slow pace so his brother could struggle along and try to keep up. While excited about shooting a real air rifle, Hans was much more anxious to play with Fritz.

Fritz met them at the door and jumped all over both boys who laughed and enjoyed the "lick fest". Chaim had his air rifle in hand and again slipped the leash on Fritz and handed it to Danny. Before they left Danny remembered their promise. He was relieved when Frau Schwartz told them she was feeling better. She thanked them for their kindness and sent them on their way. Before they rushed off she reminded them to thank their mutter for the delicious casserole. She had obviously found it the day before.

As the three boys set out for an open, abandoned field just outside of the pine forest surrounding their town, Hans gave Danny a look that was unmistakable, and Danny reluctantly handed the leash over to his brother.

When they arrived, they emptied out a bag of tin cans Chaim had collected and set them up on tree stumps and on the tops of some old boxes they found in the scrub grass. They spent the afternoon taking turns trying to out shoot each other. As with all sports, Hans took to this as a natural, and was the only one who could hit a few cans by the end of the day.

While waiting their turns to shoot, Hans and Danny took turns playing with Fritz. When Chaim waited, he barely acknowledged the loveable mass of fur vying for his attention. Chaim clearly loved his new puppy, however, he seemed more enamored with his new gun.

It was the subject of the brothers' conversation on their way home that evening. It was beyond frustrating that Chaim had this amazing dog, who he sometimes ignored, while they, who wanted a dog more than anything, couldn't have one. Hans explained that was irony, a new word he had learned the previous school year. Danny, being exceptionally bright, knew what it meant, but decided to give Hans the satisfaction of "teaching" him something for a change.

This became their new summer routine, and it was a joyous one, especially with Fritz accompanying them wherever they went. Always looking for ways to be helpful Danny had gotten some books out of the library on target shooting.

"Those little nubs on the gun are there for sighting," Danny taught Hans and Chaim.

"What's that mean?" questioned Hans.

"Well, according to this book, you're supposed to hold the gun up, level with your shoulder and lean into it. Then you align the front notch in the middle of the two rear ones and point the front one at your target." Danny showed them the illustration.

It was extremely awkward at first, but once they got the hang of it they were overjoyed to see how well that worked. Subsequently, when Chaim had trouble aiming at the targets when they were placed at a greater distance, Danny read about elevation and windage. He taught him to aim his rifle higher to account for these issues which helped Chaim tremendously. With enough practice even Danny improved, even with his terrible vision. He was pretty good at close range, but had no chance of hitting the targets at any great distance as Chaim and Hans had now mastered.

When they weren't target shooting, the boys were usually at the park with their other friends, playing baseball or football. Danny was not only very smart, he was very observant. He'd watched so many ball games from the sidelines, he'd figure out how to beat the other team and would always share his observations with his brother.

On that particular sunny afternoon Hans was playing baseball. When Danny gave Hans their secret signal, Hans did the usual; he called for a break to go 'check on Danny'.

"Henry's next at bat, so remember he always pulls to the right. You'd better put Noah in that position because Frank can't catch to save his life. Also, when it's your turn to hit, try to aim it passed Luca because he's the slowest fielder they've got and can't throw very far," Danny instructed Hans.

"Thanks, Coach," Hans smiled at his brother and ran off to take up his position on the pitcher's mound. He had taken to calling Danny, "Coach," which Danny absolutely loved. It sounded important and made him feel like part of the team.

Over the course of the summer the boys started playing War Games, which Danny considered to be an oxymoron if he'd ever heard one; but was smart enough to keep that to himself. Each team would hide a flag, which was no more than an actual rag, and the first team to capture the other team's flag won the game. When Danny saw where the opposition was hiding their flag, he'd signal his brother's team, who would inevitably win. He knew this was cheating, yet having found a way to be useful and feel included, he could easily overlook that small thing.

As the summer wore on, it became the norm for the boys to either be playing ball or shooting cans with Chaim, always with Fritz by their sides. They were all blissfully unaware of what was happening in their country. They knew from listening to their parents talk when they were supposed to be sleeping, that their Chancellor, Adolf Hitler, was promising to help all the German people by eliminating their common threat. What that threat was, the boys had no idea, nor did they really care. Their focus was on wrestling every possible moment of fun and freedom out of the waning summer days. Both Danny and Hans became masterful marksmen with Chaim's rifle, though truth be told, it was Hans who was the true marksman. They had moved the cans farther and farther away and with Danny's coaching, Hans could hit them every time at any distance. It was the most wonderful summer for Danny, for he at last had found some things he was good at, as well as finding a friend in Fritz.

## -4-

Danny had loved to read since the second grade. It made sense. Since he couldn't participate in most games, he learned to get great pleasure from reading. Reading became his passion and he had been going to Fisher Library by himself since he was in third grade. The library was only a few blocks from his house. It was a huge wood and stone structure that looked somewhat foreboding from the outside, yet inside it was warm and cozy. He had always found it to be a haven, a safe place where he could sit for hours on end and read, without anyone teasing or judging him. Danny had become good friends with the Head Librarian, Frau Zimmerman, who had taken an instant liking to the young boy. He was always polite, and there weren't many his age who preferred reading to playing outside. Of course, she realized that that wasn't an option for Danny, and she felt incredibly sympathetic towards him. She would go out of her way to find time to sit and chat with him about what he was reading. She kept a bag of candy in her desk drawer just for Danny. Danny felt very close to Frau Zimmerman and had enjoyed their relationship for many years.

On his latest trip to the library, Danny asked Frau Zimmerman to help him find books on dog training. She appeared surprised and asked, "Has your family gotten a dog?"

"Oh, I wish!" Danny exclaimed. "No, my friend just got a German Shepherd puppy, named Fritz, and I want to help teach him basic commands." They had a wonderful conversation about Frau Zimmerman's past dogs and Danny couldn't help but laugh when she described their antics.

"My favorite dog was a Labrador, named Buddy," Frau Zimmerman shared with Danny. "He was too clever for his own good! Do you know that little miscreant used to hide my shoes to get me to take him for a walk! It was only when I had his leash in hand that he would go fetch them so we could go outside! In fact, he was so smart he learned how to open the ice-box door, and one Easter he did just that...he ate the entire lamb I had prepared for Easter dinner. Would you believe we had to eat frankfurters instead?!"

"Oh I love frankfurters so that would have been fine with me," laughed Danny.

"When I lost my Buddy, I was devastated." Frau Zimmerman continued, "So after several weeks of grief, my husband came home with a little bundle. He had gotten me a German Shepherd puppy and I named her Gretel. Well! She made Buddy look like a saint! She was smart as a whip and a wonderful dog when she grew up. But, when she was a pup she seemed to have this weird fascination with toilet paper. Whenever she could get into the bathroom she'd pull it all off the roll and be covered in it when I'd find her. We'd try to keep the bathroom door closed, but she learned to open it and that was the end of the toilet paper!"

It was obvious that Frau Zimmerman had never actually gotten mad at her dogs; she clearly loved them too much.

Once Danny got home, he read several of the books and began to work with Fritz on the days when the other boys played ball. Fritz was an excellent pupil and seemed to pick everything up effortlessly. Within a month, he would sit, stay, fetch, lie down, heel and come on both voice commands as well as hand signals. Though Danny read that shepherds were the smartest breed of dog, it was still remarkable how fast Fritz learned and how eager he was to please. He had also learned that this breed was extremely protective over their masters. By six months he had grown so much that he could easily take Danny down when they wrestled, but he never hurt him. In fact, to Danny's delight, one time when Henry came over and started to push him around, as he was known to do, one growl from Fritz sent Henry swiftly on his way.

Danny noticed that Hans had started striking out at ball games, which was previously unheard of. Danny never said anything, yet he suspected it was so his brother could come over to join him in order to spend more time with Fritz. Danny would then show Hans how to give Fritz the commands that he had taught him that day.

## -5-

Over the course of the summer, Hans and Danny began eavesdropping in earnest on their parents' conversations whenever they could, and actually started paying attention when the news was on the radio. There was a lot of talk and propaganda about their leader, Adolf Hitler, around their neighborhood and they had grown increasingly curious about him. They heard their parents say that he advocated a totalitarian government, which even Danny didn't understand. They heard he was extremely anti-Semitic as well, which boggled their minds after Danny looked up what it meant. Their best friend, Chaim, was Jewish and his parents were amazing people. How could Hitler see them as a "problem"? Yet, many of their neighbors believed Hitler was good for Germany. Neither boy could come to terms with the dichotomy.

Hans and Danny talked about the fact that in school last year the students were expected to begin and end each day by standing at attention and sprouting, "Heil Hitler!" as if they meant it. If it wasn't done with the appropriate amount of enthusiasm the student was in big trouble with their teacher.

Hans told Danny, "Last year we were taught about something called racial purity."

When he saw the look of confusion on Danny's face he went on to quote his teacher, "Racial purity asserts the superiority of the Aryan race." Hans explained that they had been told that Hitler believed that the Aryan race consisted of only "pure" Germans who were better than all other races. Hans admitted he didn't know why this was true. Nevertheless that's what they had been taught.

"In addition," Hans continued, "They even replaced my favorite teacher, Herr Aaron, in the middle of the year. I heard that it was because he was Jewish! I thought that was ridiculous and figured the rumors couldn't be true."

At the time, both boys leaned towards their parents' opinions, since they trusted their judgment. Their parents had brought them up to believe in a completely different ideology. They had been lectured since birth that their loyalty was always to family first. Now in school they were told that their loyalty must be to Hitler. Their parents had taught them to treat everyone equally and fairly, so with the increasingly restrictive laws against their Jewish friends and neighbors, this didn't make sense to them.

When Hans' birthday rolled around the following week, his mutter made him his favorite dinner and baked his best-loved Kuchen, which was Donauwelle. It was a rare treat in the Wolf household because cherries were very expensive.

"Herzlichen Gluckwunsch zum Geburtstag!" They all wished Hans a happy birthday. However, still clinging to the hope that they would surprise him with his own puppy, Hans was so excited he could barely eat any of it. After dinner when they gave him his gift, his hopes were dashed. There in front of him was a long box and inside was a new baseball bat. Hans had never had his own; they always used Chaim's bat, which was fine by him. He didn't need his own bat. However, he knew how his parents must have scrimped and saved to buy him this gift, so while outwardly trying to appear happy, inside he felt angry and disheartened.

Hans secretly cursed their poverty. He loved his parents and didn't want to hurt their feelings, so he did his best to mask his true feelings. But, his thoughts went to a dark place.

While Danny had been looking forward to pouring the traditional cup of flour on top of Hans' head, he could tell Hans was very upset. Maybe Hans could fool his parents, but he couldn't fool Danny, who knew him so well. So, with great restraint and considerable disappointment, he knew enough to leave Hans alone.

Later that night, when the boys were in their shared bedroom, Hans had to vent.

"Maybe Hitler is right," he told Danny. "Why does Chaim's family have so much when we have so little? Where do you suppose they really got their money anyway? Maybe it was stolen. Maybe they aren't exactly 'the enemy,' as the Fuehrer calls them, but do they deserve to have all that money? Perhaps if we openly supported Hitler, he would live up to his promises and the wealth would be more fairly distributed."

Danny let his brother rant and waited for him to calm down before he tried to get a word in edgewise.

"Are you even listening to yourself, Hans?" Danny retorted. "Think about what you're saying. Of course our parents are right! You're just so jealous over other people's money, you're not thinking straight. You know where Chaim's family got their money. They're wonderful people who treat us like family. They are not thieves. Nor are any of the other Jewish families we've known for years. They haven't done anything wrong. The Fuehrer is just using them as scapegoats. Don't be an idiot! How can you even consider such a thing?"

Hans, angry at Danny for not understanding, yelled at him, "Never mind! You think mama and papa know everything and can't be wrong! How can so many people be saying that Hitler is right?"

"They're brainwashing you, Hans! You need to think for yourself!" Danny tried in vain to reason with his brother.

After that interaction, Hans pretty much kept his thoughts to himself, but continued to contemplate the matter privately. It was likely the most deeply he had ever thought about anything else in his life.

## -6-

During August, the boys continued with their routine. However, on several occasions, Frau Schwartz started asking Danny to stay behind when the boys went over to the park. Hans didn't know why, and he didn't care enough to ask.

Secretly Frau Schwartz felt Danny needed extra attention, so she would give him small tasks to do for her, and would reward him with praise and some coins that she told him were their secret. She was actually amazed at how quickly Danny learned and at how much Danny could do. He learned to fix fences, chop wood, and even do some house painting, which surprisingly he thoroughly enjoyed. Just as often though, Frau Schwartz would invite him to join her in the parlor where they would read side by side in quiet companionship, something they both enjoyed immensely. Danny was always offered the most comfortable chair and he could happily have stayed like that for hours. Inevitably without Danny ever noticing, so engrossed was he in what he was reading, there would appear an extra piece of chocolate torte or a pfannkuchen and a glass of milk on the small table beside his chair. He was actually disappointed when the boys showed up after their day out in the park.

The best gift of all happened on a day in late August. Next to his plate of cookies in the parlor he found an old pair of spectacles. Looking questioningly at Frau Schwartz, she smiled and explained, "They were my papa's. I don't know if they will help you with your near-sightedness, but I figured it was worth a try. I know they are not in great shape, but you're welcome to them if they will help you."

They were too big for Danny, and they had a couple of chips in the glass, as well as a small crack in one of the arms, yet it was the most wonderful thing Danny had ever been given. His own parents would never be able to afford to buy him a pair of glasses. He delicately put them on and oh mein Gott, they worked! He could see much more clearly at a distance and didn't have to scrunch up his face any more to make out anything more than ten feet away! This tiny woman was a Gott send for Danny. She enriched his life and he had no way to repay her. Uncharacteristically, he launched himself into her arms and hugged her tightly. The tears in his eyes seemed to be all the payment she would ever need.

Chaim's mutter's attention wasn't exclusively on Danny, though. She frequently commented on how handsome Hans was, with his striking eyes. She told him often he would be a lady killer when he got to be a little older, and Hans loved the attention as much as his brother. Their parents were loving and kind, however, they were never exactly generous with compliments or praise. Chaim didn't mind any of this. He was never jealous when his mama paid attention to his friends. He was a happy, easy-going child who knew he was well loved and wanted for nothing. He knew his mama had the most giving heart and the kindest of souls. She always wanted everyone she cared about to feel good about themselves, which was one of the reasons he loved her so much.

# -7-

When school started in the fall Danny braced himself for yet another year of being tortured and teased by his classmates. In fact, it was actually being encouraged by the teachers. Because of his disability, Danny was told he wasn't worthy to be one of Hitler's youths, and that he was inferior. Danny tried not to let this hurt him too much. He was aware that the teachers who were openly supportive of the Nazi regime used peer pressure to further their ideology about a superior race. Hans wouldn't be around any longer to look after him either, as Hans began his secondary education that year at a different school, called Gymnasium, while Danny had another few years at the primary school, Volksschule.

On the other hand, Hans was secretly looking forward to going back to school because Lilly Wagner was in his class that year. He had a crush on her for over a year now, but was too afraid of rejection to even talk to her. She was the prettiest girl in their school and usually hung out with the upper classmen. Hans suspected he would probably get beaten up by these bigger boys if he even tried to get too close to her, so he kept his distance and pined over her. He was determined to get his courage up, which normally wasn't a problem for him. Then again, he had never liked a girl before. Where he'd take on a kind twice his size if they were bullying Danny or Chaim, this was different. Whenever he was near Lilly he got tongue-tied and would begin to sweat. She was from a prominent German family and that, too, did nothing to lift his confidence.

The year progressed as expected, although Danny's classmates weren't quite as cruel as he had anticipated....maybe they had finally gotten tired of torturing him, he hoped. Perhaps at age twelve his quick mind was finally a thing to be admired rather than ridiculed along with his bum foot. While Hans struggled in all his subjects, Danny excelled.

About halfway through the year, in January, 1938, young men, boys really, started showing up at Hans' school in swastika emblazoned uniforms calling themselves SS officers, working for their commandant, Adolf Hitler. Hans couldn't figure out why, but all the girls, Lilly included, seemed to find them irresistible. They seemed to convey power and authority. He had no idea what their jobs really were or why they were appearing out of the blue to wander the halls of Becker Secondary School, or hang out on its grounds, seemingly without purpose. The young officers did, however, seem to enjoy pushing around some of the weaker students, and Gott help any of his Jewish friends if they got noticed. By this time Hans still hadn't gotten the nerve to speak to Lilly, and she was a constant distraction for him in his classes as he daydreamed and fancied himself her boyfriend. Perhaps, he considered, if he wore one of those uniforms she'd pay attention to him.

In fact, he secretly admired these SS officers who seemed to have the attention of every girl in his grade. He even recognized some of them. He spotted Henry's older brother, Liam, hanging around at their school. Liam used to be a scrawny boy like Hans. Now he had certainly bulked up. He was muscular and looked strong and fit. He also looked arrogant, but that was nothing new. No wonder the girls were attracted to these young men, he thought.

It was only a few weeks later, after listening in once again on his parents' now tense conversations, that Hans learned what was going on in his native country. Their leader, who had come to power in those turbulent times of poverty and strife, was trying to pull his nation together by identifying and eliminating their common enemy: anyone who was Jewish, or who wasn't pure German. Hans found this laughable. All his Polish and Jewish neighbors were good, hard-working people. What on earth could they have done to have become 'the enemy,' the reason for all that plagued their country? How could anyone in their right mind believe such nonsense? However, his parents seemed to take this man seriously and worried in hushed voices about their friends and the threat of war. Hans suspected that would never come to pass.

## -8-

On a brutally cold day in late January, Chaim was heading to their meeting place after school to walk home with Hans, Henry, Noah and Frank. Being overweight had always been a source of teasing for Chaim. And it was again, or at least that's how it started. Two of the SS officers, who were now a common sight on campus, began to follow him extremely closely. They called him unpleasant names, perhaps more vile and harsh than he had heard before. This bordered more on bullying than teasing. Chaim handled it as he had in the past and chose to ignore them.

This, however, proved to be the wrong course of action. The officers believed no one had the right to ignore them. They thought of themselves as part of Hitler's regime, and therefore commanded respect and obedience from everyone else. This boy had no right to ignore them! The larger of the two grabbed Chaim by the shoulder, spun him around, and demanded to know his name. Starting to realize his danger, Chaim became paralyzed with fear. Everyone knew these officers hated Jews. He became tongue-tied, not knowing what to say or do. He certainly didn't want to tell them his name as that would give him away. The smaller officer snatched his book bag and emptied its contents onto the sidewalk, kicking things around with his boot. He opened one of Chaim's notebooks and saw his name printed on the inside cover, clear as day. With that, their torment started in earnest. The officers were thrilled to have a Jew to beat up.

Meanwhile, Chaim's friends were growing impatient waiting for him. Fortunately for Chaim, they had become concerned and started back to the school to find him. They intervened just in time. Chaim had already taken several hard punches to his stomach and had been knocked to the ground, but he hadn't yet been seriously injured.

When the four boys showed up, Hans quickly analyzed the situation and didn't even hesitate to walk right up to the officers and say, "I think there must have been a misunderstanding here. This is our good friend, Ben Deutsch."

While the officers knew that was a lie, they also knew they were gravely outnumbered. The officers, being the cowards they really were, chose to accept this information as valid and walked away. Chaim had never been more grateful to Hans, or happier to see his friends in his life, which he suspected might have been forfeited if they hadn't shown up when they did.

When Hans shared this event with his family that evening, he could see a mixture of pride and concern in his parents' eyes. They told him he did the right thing, and then advised him to try to stay clear of all SS officers in the future.

Danny was really proud of his brother as well. He knew Hans would defend their friend, as Hans' loyalty was his best quality and was never in question. Danny was impressed that Hans had figured out exactly the right thing to say to disarm the situation. Perhaps he hadn't been giving Hans enough credit in the brains department.

Danny smiled at his brother and praised him, "Way to go, Hans. You were never afraid to stand up to bullies. You really handled that situation well."

Hans smiled back and reveled in the rare praise from his brother.

When Hans was alone in his room, he relived the event in his head. Of course, he had stood up for Chaim...there wasn't any choice in the matter, he thought. He knew in his heart he had done the right thing, but maybe this was being blown out of proportion. Danny was probably right, as usual, the SS officers did seem to be bullies. But, that didn't mean they were following Hitler's orders. Perhaps, they had just been taking advantage of their position. Chaim hadn't really been hurt, right? Hans just couldn't seem to see past the prestige that these officers emanated. His head hurt from thinking so much, and all he knew was that he was still ambivalent about SS officers.

# -9-

In early February, all the boys aged 16 – 18 who were deemed worthy by virtue of their racial purity, health, and leadership abilities, were called into a special assembly at Becker Secondary School where the SS officers presided. They were recruiting for new officers and as they spoke they made it seem like the only course of action for the students to take if they cared about their country. They painted a picture of living in luxury and commanding respect and obedience wherever they went, as they had been trained to say. Hans craved the life they described. He was tired of being poor and of watching the girl of his dreams swayed by these uniforms. If he had money he could finally get his own dog. Yet, they were calling his neighbors terrible things and calling for their actual removal from their communities to establish peace. While being impoverished was sadly their way of life, it had indeed always been a peaceful community. His Jewish and Polish neighbors could not possibly be considered 'evil' by any stretch of the imagination. Hans' thoughts were at war, not knowing what to believe. Yet, he certainly felt swayed to become one of these officers. Who wouldn't crave that prestige?

That night at dinner Hans shared what had happened at school that day. His parents were appalled that they hadn't been notified as they would never have given permission for Hans to attend; though they suspected that was the idea. Their permission wasn't wanted or needed. If their son hadn't attended, would they too become "the enemy within?" These were unprecedented times and caution seemed to be the prudent course of action. In fact, Herr and Frau Wolf had heard that the Nazis had even taken over the administration and changed the curriculum at all the secondary schools. They had learned that Hitler was trying to cultivate a loyal following of young men and used the curriculum as an indoctrination process, which the Wolfs felt was more like brainwashing. Jacob and Emma looked at each other and knew they'd be having a long talk after the boys went to bed.

To their utter dismay, Hans continued to talk about the glory of becoming an SS officer.

"Just think about it. If I were an officer I would be well paid and could support the family. Papa wouldn't have to work at that factory he hates so much. If I was an officer I could protect all of us so much easier. They may even give me a dog to use to patrol the community."

These were all the ideas he had come up with on his way home from school in hopes of persuading his parents. Training to be an SS officer also held great appeal for Hans as school work certainly wasn't his strength, to which his failing grades could attest each year. Of course, he didn't admit that, or the fact that trying to impress LIlly was also part of the appeal.

While his parents sat in stunned silence, it was Danny who vehemently argued with his brother and didn't hesitate to call him an ass, among other unattractive names, for even considering such a thing.

"I can't believe my own brother would join up with those arrogant bullies!" Danny confronted Hans in disbelief.

"They're not all bullies, Danny, and they are serving our nation. Shouldn't we be doing that as well?" Hans countered.

"Hans, are you blind as well as dumb? I've been bullied all my life. Don't you think I know one when I see one?! They treat anyone who isn't pure German at best with disdain, if not outright hostility. You were there…you saw what they did to Chaim! You couldn't possibly have forgotten that!" Danny suspected Hans had not, but chose to see it in his own light. He felt as if this person sitting across from him was a stranger. An alien must have replaced his brother. There was no other reasonable explanation for it!

Herr Wolf gently chastised Danny for his inappropriate language, even though he agreed whole-heartedly with him. What had come over his oldest son? He knew this was a crucial moment and looked to his wife for support on how to handle this. If they adamantly forbade it, would it actually push Hans to pursue this crazy idea? He knew boys of Hans' age often became belligerent and defiant.

Fortunately, Emma came to the rescue. In her gentle, most rational voice she tried to reason with Hans. "Hans, sweetheart, I know it's confusing because you're hearing different things from different adults, all of whom you've been taught to trust. Honey, please listen to me. You know I only want the best for you. The Fuehrer has a very large, loyal following and they have been trained to tell you certain things that are not true. Hitler is not what the news has made him out to be. He has a misguided ideology in his hate for all but the Aryan people, and I fear that will only lead us all into a great war. I know he is revered by many, but he truly is a madman who is intent on eliminating all the good Polish and Jewish people we know."

Of course, Hans didn't want to hear any of this and stood up suddenly stating, "I'm not hungry. May I be excused?"

Not wanting to pursue it at that juncture, his vater agreed. Jacob needed time to think and talk to Emma about what to do. Was this just a passing trend or was this as serious as it sounded?

Danny persisted in trying to reason with his brother after they had gone to bed. "Hans, those SS officers are trying to brainwash you with their persuasive lies. I get what you are saying, but you've got to trust our parents, not the propaganda that's being pandered as gospel by these Nazis!"

At this point Hans was refusing to even acknowledge his existence, except to routinely tell him to shut up.

"Danny, you don't know as much as you think you do. You love to throw big words around to make yourself seem smart, but you weren't at the meetings and don't understand what you're talking about. So just shut up already!" Hans seethed, barely able to contain his anger and frustration.

When Danny continued to bombard him with his version of logic, Hans finally lost control and did the unthinkable. He actually shoved Danny so hard that he hit the wall and collapsed onto their bedroom floor; a look of horror and shock emanating from Danny's eyes.

"I guess I will shut up," Danny whispered. "You have clearly already become one of them."

# -10-

In March, there were further meetings at the middle school. Instead of being led by SS officers, they were led by their commanders, who were certainly more persuasive, as well as quite ominous. They inferred that anyone not with them was against them, and therefore their enemy as well. Anyone who purposely aided any Jews or Poles would also meet with their same fate. What that fate was, the young adults could only try to imagine.

It was a dreadfully strained time in the Wolf home as well as throughout their community. It seemed everyone was taking sides. Out of fear, or out of actual belief that Hitler would make their world better, most of the Germans sided with Hitler.

It was in April that it happened. The Wolf brothers were still barely speaking to each other and the tension this created in the household was being felt by all. Nevertheless, at their vater's insistence, Hans was still required to walk Danny to primary school before he and Chaim continued on to their new school. When they got to Chaim's house to pick him up, it was evident that something terrible had happened. The front screen door was hanging off its hinges and the main door was swung open. As the boys approached they could see only chaos. The once beautiful home was in shambles. Tables were overturned and broken, glass was shattered, and their belongings were strewn over the floor. It was also obvious upon further investigation that most of their priceless antiques were missing. While terrified, the boys couldn't look away. They were suddenly a unified force searching for their friend. It was clear that the house was now deserted. At first they called for Chaim in whispers. However, as their panic increased, so did their voices. Still, there was no answer, only silence and destruction.

Just then a sudden sound arose from the basement. Both boys jumped at least a foot into the air, which spoke to their level of alarm. They grabbed onto each other for support and listened. Then it came again, unmistakable this time. It was a whimpering…it had to be Fritz! Hans raced to the basement with Danny limping along at his heels. Sure enough, they found Fritz locked in a closet, alone and scared. When he saw the boys he could barely be contained, so happy was he to see their friendly, beloved faces. Without a word spoken, the boys led Fritz up and out of the house and headed towards home, towards relative safety.

When Emma saw the boys and the dog, she immediately suspected the worst and gathered them up in her arms, where they willingly stayed for several minutes. Hans told her the Schwartz's home had been robbed and vandalized. Danny looked at his brother in astonishment. Did he really believe that?

Danny looked straight into his mutter's eyes and told her the last thing she wanted to hear. "It was the Nazis," he told her. "If it was burglars, where was the family?" He had half expected to find them bound and gagged downstairs with Fritz, but that hope died as soon as they had entered the room. It was only Fritz left behind.

Emma sent the boys to their room. She wished she could get in touch with Jacob. She could do nothing except wait anxiously all afternoon, wringing her hands and worrying. Jacob would know what to do, she kept assuring herself. It would all be okay.

But, at 6:00 when Jacob finally arrived home and heard what had happened, he too had no idea what to do. He had always relied on his wife's wisdom and common sense when it came to anything of great magnitude in their lives. While theoretically he wore the pants in the family, as was expected in their culture, they had always been a team and conferred on everything of consequence. In this instance though, neither one knew what could be done. They suspected Chaim's family had been taken away as others had before them. They had no clue as to where that might be. There were rumors of horrific places called concentration camps, and feared that Danny had been right...it had to have been the Nazis who did this.

This calamity in their tight-knit community drove it home. This war of discrimination had reached their door. Did they have the gumption to stand up for what was right, what was just? Or did they, as so many before them, just bow down and let it happen in order to save their own lives. Really, what could they do?

## -11-

Suffering in silence, the Wolfs realized that their only course of action was no action at all. While hating themselves for doing it, they continued to go through their days as if nothing had happened. While ashamed, their fear for their family's safety trumped their natural desire to do the right thing.

Unaware that the boys were listening, Emma and Jacob began talking nightly about moving to America. They had no idea how they would manage it, but it gave them hope to dream of a better life. It gave them something to strive for, and they'd talk about how they could tighten their budget even more to start saving for this costly endeavor.

Hans and Danny discussed how they felt about that possibility. They were clearly conflicted, as this was the only life they knew and were uncomfortable leaving it behind. Yet, the thought of moving to a new, safe land of opportunity, as they'd heard it described, was indeed enticing.

To the boys' secret delight though, keeping Fritz was never even brought into question. They didn't know where their parents were getting the money, especially now that they were trying to save even more, but Fritz was always fed and looked after as if he had always been part of their family. It was Danny who figured it out. It was his parents' way of consoling themselves. At least they were taking care of the Schwartz's beloved pet. And Fritz, having already been well trained by Danny, gave the family no trouble at all. He was clearly grateful to join this loving family with not one, but two boys who fawned over him and snuck him treats whenever they could. For some reason, to Danny's consternation though, Fritz seemed to bond with Hans above anyone else. He never let Hans out of his sight. Danny wondered if Fritz was attracted to the suppressed nervous energy that always seemed to emanate from Hans.

On the following day Frau Wolf suggested that it may be wiser to keep Fritz at home when they went off to their weekend ball games. But, Fritz would have no part of that. After jumping the fence on three occasions to follow them, Danny was asked if he could train Fritz not to do that. Danny got a kick out of Fritz following them. However, always being the obedient son, he complied with his parents' wishes. He always felt the unspoken pressure to make up for Hans' lack of compliance. While he often silently resented this, it was just the way it was. Danny always acquiesced to his parents' wishes.

Having gained quite the skill as a dog trainer, it posed no problem for Danny. However, it seemed that everyone underestimated Fritz's ingenuity and determination. He wouldn't disobey one of his masters. He wouldn't jump the fence. Instead he learned how to unlatch the gate and follow them without breaking any rules. Herr Wolf was thinking that he could tie the gate closed with rope, however that posed a problem for the family coming and going, and Gott knew they couldn't afford to buy a lock for the gate. So the Wolfs decided maybe it wasn't such a bad idea for Fritz to accompany their sons. He had grown into a large, powerful animal who, they suspected, would attack anyone who threatened his boys.

As it turned out, the Wolfs were correct. The following weekend at a game of football when Henry tackled Hans savagely to the ground, it took mere seconds for Fritz to spring into action. Having been playing with Danny on the sidelines, he had nevertheless kept an eye on his beloved Hans. When Henry heard the menacing growl and felt Fritz's hot breath in his ear, he froze, paralyzed with fear. Hans quickly tapped out and called Fritz off, yelling, "Platz! Bleib!" Fritz immediately obeyed, lying down and staying still. For a second Hans had actually been afraid that Fritz might attack his friend. Now that it was over, he couldn't resist a small smile of satisfaction knowing that Fritz had his back. That was nothing compared to Danny, who was practically jumping for joy, happy that Henry, the biggest bully in their circle, had been brought to his knees.

Later that night, at dinner when the boys shared their story, Emma and Jacob actually breathed a small sigh of relief. Fritz was worth every penny they spent on him and more. But, Fritz couldn't be everywhere. Recruitment meetings continued on a monthly basis at Becker Secondary School. Hans was required to attend, and as he listened he became more and more enamored with the prospect of becoming an SS soldier. He chose to believe it wasn't the Nazis who had destroyed Chaim's house. Everything bad that happened was being blamed on the Nazis. Hans believed that the Schwartz family was smart and recognized the threat in time. He convinced himself that they had fled in the dead of night to leave Germany and seek passage to the Americas.

Many rumors circulating in the neighborhood supported this belief, but Danny suspected they were made up because the alternative was too hard to accept. He was sure Hans secretly prayed that the rumors were true. Danny kept telling

Hans that it was pretty amazing what nonsense he had convinced himself to believe whenever Hans shared his thoughts with him.

He tried again to get Hans to listen to reason.

"Chaim would have confided in us if they were going to move, Hans. Surely you must know that. He wouldn't have left the country without telling us and would never have left Fritz locked in a closet!" Danny pointed out. To this Hans had no retort.

So, Danny continued, "How do you explain the destruction and all the missing treasures? You have to admit that doesn't make any sense. They certainly couldn't have carried the portraits and their fancy furniture onto a ship. It had to be the Nazis who stole it all. Or maybe the Nazis told Chaim's family to bring their most prized possessions with them for some reason. Maybe they were told they could use them to barter for other necessities."

This time Hans responded, "Yeah, perhaps they traded their valuables for passage to America, and then maybe the house was ransacked by burglars afterwards." This sounded lame even to his own ears, so he went on trying to make sense of it all. "You know Frau Schwartz had all that expensive jewelry she could have used to trade for passage."

Everyone knew about Frau Schwartz's jewelry, particularly her diamond encrusted brooch that had been her mutter's. She was especially fond of that piece and wore it almost daily. Her gems had often been the talk of the neighborhood, and Hans suspected that even his mutter, who was normally practical and sensible, secretly envied those magnificent jewels.

"Ok, let me get this straight...so you think that they bartered all their valuables, including the jewelry, to pay for passage to America, without telling us, and then left in the dead of night, and then burglars happened to come that same night and couldn't find anything of value so they destroyed the house out of spite?" Danny mocked Hans' ideas.

"Well, when you put it like that, it does sound far-fetched. But, you're jumping to conclusions, too!"

Danny knew that Hans would continue to believe what he wanted to believe to the unending frustration of the rest of his family.

In early June of 1938, at the last assembly of the school year, the boys at Becker Secondary School were addressed by one of Hitler's SS-Obergruppenfuhrers, one of the highest ranking officers in his regime. His authoritative manner was intimidating and the boys sat up attentively. Many even held their breath.

"You are all now men," he spoke in a commanding manner. "You no longer need the permission or support of your families to make the right choice. You've been instructed that your loyalty is to Hitler. It is now time for you to stand up and be brave. It is time for you to serve your country. You must make your decision. Do you want to become an esteemed SS officer or be a coward? Over the course of the summer you will be visited by officers who will expect you to be ready to join our regime. You will be trained to fight against the evil that plagues our country. This is your moral duty and your obligation. I fully expect every one of you to show your loyalty to our great leader."

The SS-Obergruppenfuhrer continued to remind them emphatically of their duty in no uncertain terms. It was obvious, even to Hans, that there really wasn't much of a choice. They were led to believe that if they didn't join voluntarily, they had cause to worry about their futures. It was all black and white – join or perish.

Hans knew what his decision was going to be, what it had to be. He knew what he would do to protect his family – which was how he chose to see it. It was his job now to watch out for his family, and with the power that came with the uniform, he'd be able to do just that.

Later that night, while lying in bed, Hans shared with Danny everything they had been told at the assembly and what he was planning to do. They had finally started talking again. Hans had stopped telling his parents about the school assemblies because he knew they would never tolerate what he was going to do. However, he felt compelled to confide in someone. He didn't know why he talked to Danny though, because they were never of like mind. Danny kept telling him that it was amazing what nonsense he had convinced himself to believe whenever Hans shared his thoughts. Danny reminded Hans that he didn't need to make such a drastic choice since their parents were trying to seek passage to America.

To this however, Hans replied, "Danny, it would be great, but you know our family will never have enough money to do that." Danny couldn't realistically argue that point.

Danny suspected Hans' motives to join Hitler's youths weren't as noble as he tried to make them sound. Danny knew Hans secretly admired the uniforms and the attention they got from the girls, especially Lilly. While Hans had never confided his affection for that particular girl, Danny knew how Hans felt about her. He had recently read Hans' journal, a transgression of which he wasn't proud. He felt it was necessary at that time.

When Hans wasn't talking to him he was desperate to know what Hans was contemplating. Danny knew that Hans had been keeping a journal for years, and even if he hadn't read about it, it was pretty obvious by the way he'd stare at Lilly whenever she was near. And where Danny saw the SS officers as a bunch of bullies, Hans saw power and prestige, which Danny knew Hans privately craved. Hans had never been bullied, and while he had intervened on Danny's behalf when it would get too hostile, he himself had never experienced the humiliation and pain Danny had suffered most of his life. Hans just couldn't understand what it was like. He knew Hans yearned for the status and the power these officers seemed to emanate.

Mostly Danny feared for Hans' safety. If what Hans was saying was true, he'd be leaving their family shortly and going Gott only knew where and for how long. While Hans was on the cusp of his 17$^{th}$ birthday, he was still a kind in Danny's eyes. As angry as he was with his brother, he couldn't imagine life without him. Why did the Fuehrer want kinder in his army anyway? It didn't make sense to him. Danny hated Hitler vehemently and continued to blame him for the disappearance of Chaim's family.

However, once school ended, the following weeks could only be described as bliss for Danny. Hans became the perfect brother. He was nicer to Danny than he had ever been and wanted to spend time with him like never before. They spent hours playing with Fritz and teaching him new commands. They even tossed the ball around, just the two of them, with Fritz playing the monkey in the middle. When Hans asked Danny to take good care of Fritz when he was gone, Danny was filled with an equal measure of delight and grief; delight in having Fritz to himself, and grief over Hans leaving.

Hans had even begun to do his chores without being told several times as had been his norm. Hans surprised even himself when he started helping his mama in the kitchen, which he had always considered to be "woman's work." Danny, who had turned thirteen was very mature for his age and knew this was Hans' way of showing how much he really loved his family and how much he was going to miss them.

With each passing day the dread grew because, from what Hans had shared, it was just a matter of time, and not much of that either. Danny kept his promise not to tell his parents, though he ached to do so. He couldn't understand how Hans wasn't even giving them a warning that he would not only be leaving them soon, but joining up with an army that his parents covertly despised. He tried to give Hans the benefit of the doubt, but privately he thought he was taking the coward's way out. Rather than have to face his parents' anguish and heartbreak, as well as their vain attempts to talk him out of it, he would just up and leave. Danny suspected his parents would have found a way to move to America to keep their family together and safe, if they knew what Hans was planning. However, Danny bit his tongue. He couldn't betray Hans. He loved him and didn't want to fight with him anymore. If Hans had his mind made up, as he clearly did, he wanted their last days together to be as idyllic as possible.

# -12-

It was August 27<sup>th</sup> when it finally happened. It's too soon Danny thought as panic swept through him. Through the living room window he saw two SS officers walking up the path to their door. They didn't knock on the door. They banged three times showing off their authority. It was a Saturday and Herr Wolf came to the door and could only stare in shock at the officers. Without asking, they entered the house and pushed past Jacob knocking him aside in the process. Danny knew it wasn't accidental, but was wary enough to keep his mouth closed when all he wanted to do was launch himself at the strangers who pushed his vater around like he was nothing. Danny wasn't the only witness, and when Fritz growled and prepared to lunge at the officer who had dared touch one of his family, Danny swiftly clutched his collar and issued an urgent command to stay. One of the SS officers had actually reached for his sidearm when he spotted the huge shepherd. Herr Wolf immediately instructed Danny to take Fritz outside for fear of what might happen. The taller of the two men spoke loudly, as if he was addressing a large audience, and stated they had come to see Hans Wolf and hear his decision.

Scrambling to understand what was transpiring, Jacob finally realized the significance of this unexpected visit. He was overcome with horror and a need to protect his oldest son. As he was about to order these impertinent soldiers out of his house, Hans came into the room with a knapsack slung over his shoulder, and Jacob knew there was nothing he could do to stop the inevitable. He should have suspected something was amiss over the last couple of weeks when Hans had inexplicably turned into the "perfect" child. Instead, he had just enjoyed the unexpected pleasure of seeing his sons getting along famously. Stunned and frozen in place he saw Emma enter the room. The shock and terror on her face tore him apart. She too had deduced what was about to happen. Hans asked the SS officers to give him a few moments alone with his family before he joined them outside, where he could see at least a dozen of his former classmates lined up with their knapsacks. A look of gloom and despair was evident on most of their young faces. The officers complied, but not without a filthy remark slipping out loudly enough to be heard as they exited their home. "Mieze," Danny heard one of them say and cringed. He had left Fritz outside and quietly reentered the house. Here was his brother bravely leaving his home and family and these bastards could only humiliate him for caring for his family.

    Before either parent could find their voice, Hans quickly and succinctly told them, "I'm sorry you don't approve of my decision, but it is mine to make. I love you all, but I firmly believe that this will be best for all of us." He couldn't look them in the eyes because he knew those loving eyes would be filled with tears and compassion. Hans knew that would tear him apart and weaken his resolve. Trying to keep his own tears in check he hugged each parent in turn and told them, "Don't worry about me. I will stay in touch and I will be okay." Lastly, he hugged his brother, and Danny never wanted it to end. Danny wished his brother luck and, unable to contain his own tears, quickly turned away.

Without a backward glance Hans was gone. Emma's legs gave way and she crumbled to the floor weeping hysterically. Jacob got down on the floor with her, folded her in his arms and wept alongside his wife. Danny, immersed in his own loss and grief, stood helplessly to the side not knowing what to do. After what felt like an eternity, he turned and was out the back door and out of the yard with Fritz by his side. He walked for hours, his bum foot throbbing in agony, first crying, then screaming, and then lapsing back into silence. Danny was beyond caring what anyone who saw him thought....knowing that there were at least a dozen other families in his neighborhood who were going through the same hell as they were. Finally, when he could take the pain no longer he limped home to find his parents on the couch still wrapped in each other's arms, their faces tear stained, and their eyes red and swollen. They somehow seemed smaller, shrunken by the weight of their loss. Without a word they opened their arms and Danny fell into them like a life net. He had no idea how long they were there. The shadows had grown long and they all felt hollowed out and empty inside. Fritz, seeming to understand the situation, lay at their feet quietly, lost in his own sorrow. Where was Hans? Why hadn't Hans taken him along? When would he be back?

When at last Emma sat up, she looked at Danny and said softly, "You knew, didn't you? Why didn't you stop him?"

His mama's words cut deep and Danny frantically tried to come up with a response. He couldn't find a way to explain how much he had suffered keeping his brother's confidence and how much he had wanted to tell them. Instead he hung his head guiltily and that was enough. Emma somehow pulled herself together and said she would go make them dinner. She needed to keep busy and not dwell on what would otherwise have sent her screaming into the night, not unlike what Danny had done earlier that evening.

Over dinner, when Danny expected the conversation to be all about Hans and their concern for his welfare, it was a shock that his parents didn't say a word about him. Not once was his name brought up, not once was their pain on display again. This was, Danny knew, his parents' way of coping. It made him want to burst. He wanted to assure them that Hans would be fine. He would be trained and well cared for as the other officers seemed to have been. He needed to believe this himself. Even though Hans had done the unthinkable in their minds, all that mattered was that he would come home to them safe and sound.

That night, after Danny had climbed wearily into bed, his mama knocked softly on his door. Upon entering, she came over and sat on the side of Danny's small bed and stroked his hair, something she hadn't done in many years. Her eyes were still red and she seemed to have shrunken even further from this new burden she would somehow have to bear.

She spoke softly, "Danny, I'm very sorry for what I said earlier this evening." With a small, sad smile she told Danny, "I know you could no more have stopped Hans from leaving than you could have stopped the wind from blowing or the rain from falling."

Danny was comforted by her words. "I wanted to tell you so badly, but I promised Hans I would keep his secret. I know he didn't want to hurt you. I tried to talk him out of it, but he wouldn't listen to reason."

Trying to make her son feel better, Emma whispered, "Hans has always been a bit hard-headed, wouldn't you agree?" This poor attempt at humor actually did bring a smile to Danny's lips, as he remembered literally hundreds of times over their lifetimes when he couldn't talk Hans out of doing something stupid.

Emma hugged Danny tightly and told him everything would be okay. Danny wished he could believe her, but the sparkle in his mama's eyes was gone, which told him more than her words could convey.

## -13-
## Danny

For Danny, life became unbearable in the Wolf household over the next month. He wanted his parents to find a way to get in touch with Hans to find out how he was making out. But, they wouldn't even discuss Hans with him. Little did he know that both his parents were frantically making furtive inquiries to find out whatever they could, which sadly amounted to nothing. There was apparently to be no contact from the outside. These young men were being trained to be soldiers and any form of coddling or family interaction was strictly prohibited. They were being taught duty above all else, where both boys had always been raised to believe it was supposed to be family above all else.

When other Jewish and Polish families went missing, there was to be no discussion about them, so paranoid had everyone become. Rumors were that if you even whispered anything negative about the Fuehrer, you would be targeted next. Little by little Danny's community shrank and became clandestine in their actions.

While Danny expected it to be his mutter, it was actually his vater who seemed to be the most affected by everything happening around them. Privately Jacob cursed himself for not having seen the signs, for not getting his family out of Germany before it was too late. Even if they had the money now, they could never leave without Hans. Jacob hated himself for working in a factory that made weapons that supported the war efforts. He couldn't bring himself to comprehend why the war was even being waged. The only reason for violence, in his mind, was if his family's lives were being threatened. Instead all he could see was their "esteemed" leader threatening the lives of innocent, hard-working people, whose only "sin" appeared to be that they weren't born German. The only way for Jacob to get through his days was not to think about how the weapons he was helping to produce would be used. While Emma suffered silently, Jacob took to taking long lonely walks after dinner, mumbling to himself as he walked, totally oblivious of anyone around him. The remaining neighbors, perhaps suffering as well, seemed to take pity on Jacob and would ask him into their homes for a cup of tea. Jacob barely acknowledged the kind offers, preferring his loneliness to company.

Late at night, Danny would hear his mama's muffled sobs and prayers to an unheeding Gott to bring her son back to them. He could hear his papa offering empty comfort. Sometimes he'd hear his papa's angry tirade, berating himself for not having done better for the family. At this point his mama would, in turn, try to comfort him, telling him not to blame himself and it wasn't his fault. Danny started falling asleep with a pillow over his head to block out the conversations. They hurt too deeply and Danny knew no way to console his parents.

# -14-
# Hans

On that hot day in August when Hans and his comrades were marched off into the unknown, Hans had vowed to himself that he would make his family proud. He would become a fine soldier and help Hitler bring peace to Germany. The fact that there was peace before Hitler, and that now they were in an incomprehensible war seemed to escape Hans entirely. They were herded onto buses and brought to a training facility a few hours away. Upon arrival the new recruits weren't exactly treated with hostility, but with derision. The older officers seemed to take delight in pushing them around.

Hans and the other trainees were put in B 27, a long, drafty, dimly lit barracks where they were given a bunk and a tiny metal closet to store their meager belongings. Anything of value was quickly confiscated and they were issued uniforms, boots and weapons. They were given their own rifles and handguns and the training began almost immediately upon arrival. The wake up bugle sounded promptly at 5:00 am every morning. They were marched for hours in every kind of weather, being forced to carry great weight on their backs the whole time. Smoldering heat or torrential rains were apparently no reason for a "day off." The boys murmured among themselves once lights were out at night, and some even cried into their pillows. What had they gotten themselves into? They all suffered foot sores, cramps, and aching muscles, but mostly heartache. Every night Hans would spend about ten minutes writing in his journal. Writing helped him to deal with the reality of the situation. His language teacher way back in fifth grade had taught him this was cathartic. He had tried it back then and it had helped. He had started using his journal to help himself deal with his emotions, and he had never stopped.

Not surprisingly though, when the weapons training began, Hans started to find he enjoyed every moment of it. He had been self-taught along with Chaim and his brother, and this indeed helped him succeed. While shooting a MP 40 submachine gun was way different from shooting an air rifle, Hans had already learned the basics; how to sight down a rifle, as well as how to take windage into account. Hans knew how to elevate his weapon when needed. Danny had taught him all that what now seemed to be a lifetime ago. Weighing about nine pounds, the weapon was significantly heavier than the air rifle he had been used to firing. It was fully automatic but its relatively slow rate of fire enabled it to be a single shot gun with a controlled trigger pull. It chambered thirty-two 9 mm rounds.

Hans was fascinated by the weapon and even took it upon himself to practice his aim in his free time, which impressed his superiors and improved his skills remarkably. While none of the other boys could hit the side of a barn in broad daylight, Hans could hit a target easily at 100 yards out. His commanders took notice and suddenly he was the golden boy. They themselves couldn't even match Hans' marksmanship. The Nazis had always relied on sheer numbers in combat, rather than true marksmanship. They hadn't bothered to learn what had now become second nature to Hans.

Hans was taken from his damp quarters and moved to a more "luxurious" barracks where at least there were fans blowing in the hot weather, heat in the cold weather, brighter lights, and much, much better food. He took to all the weapons training as if he had been doing it all his life and this brought him much praise from his superiors. In B 17, his new barracks, he found his old friend, Henry, who smoothed the way to his acceptance by the other boys already there.

Hans was eventually put on an elite squad, which made him proud. Finally, he excelled at something that seemed to matter. That was until it slowly dawned on him why he was being trained so thoroughly in combat.

"Had I really been that naïve?" he chastised himself. This wasn't fun and games. He was being trained to kill innocent people... had that really escaped him?

## -15-
## Danny

It was the end of September and life had become a torturous routine back at the Wolf residence. The family went through their days in a daze. The life and joy seemed to have been sucked out of their once warm, loving household the day Hans left. While Danny missed his brother terribly, he was angry with him as well.

He told Fritz, "I know you loved him too, but look what Hans has done to our parents. They haven't been themselves since he left. He was obviously too blind to see what he was doing. You'd think all those dinner conversations about the horrors that were being inflicted on our friends and neighbors would have given Hans more common sense. Sadly, that's something he has always lacked. It's one thing to destroy his own life, but now he's destroying mine as well. Mama and Papa barely seem to take notice of me anymore. It's a good thing I have you to talk to. You're a really good listener." Danny hugged Fritz tightly and ruffled his soft fur. Fritz whined sympathetically as if he understood what Danny was saying.

Danny's mutter still provided hot meals and his vater continued to labor at the factory, yet he couldn't even remember a smile or a word of encouragement from them since that August day. He resented the neglect and decided to act on it.

Danny took to leaving after dinner with Fritz, without saying where they were going or when they'd be back. They usually went off to the park, where they used to be young, innocent and free. He'd sit and read with Fritz by his side, wishing they could go back in time.

Danny also spent a lot more time at the library. Frau Zimmerman had no problem allowing a dog into her beloved library. In fact, she looked forward to his visits, and started keeping a bag of biscuits next to the candy that she reserved for Danny. She no longer had a dog and enjoyed Fritz's company as much as Danny's.

Frau Zimmerman told Danny, "It's amazing how much Fritz looks like my Gretel. They're both sable colored with beautiful black masks. Even the black fur on their backs is more of a blanket than a saddle, and their fur is longer and softer than most shepherds. Fritz is quite a bit larger than she was though, and Gretel certainly couldn't do any of the tricks that Fritz can do. I'm so impressed with what you've taught him!"

In an effort to please her, Danny taught Fritz to pick up any fallen object on command. He knew Frau Zimmerman had a lot of back pain and wanted to help her in any way he could. She had never complained to him, but he'd seen her wince on many occasions when she had to bend over. As anticipated, Frau Z, as Danny had come to call her, was indeed delighted with this! She would drop things on purpose, just so Fritz could show off.

Danny's parents had kept him home from school that year, not wanting him to experience any Nazi indoctrination, and Emma had begun to homeschool him. While they knew he would never be recruited with his club foot, they still felt it was for the best. They wanted to keep a low profile, fearing the rumors they heard about mandatory sterilization of anyone with a physical or mental disability. Emma and Jacob had learned that all Jewish teachers had been fired, or worse, and were replaced by Nazi appointments based on political reliability rather than on competency. They had also heard that the curriculum now focused almost entirely on the Nazi's beliefs, such as racial hygiene. They felt Danny wouldn't have learned anything of importance at school and was safer at home.

Without contact with other students, and with Hans and Chaim gone, Danny was incredibly lonely. His parents were essentially "absent" as well, if not in body, definitely in spirit. He didn't think he could have endured his life if it hadn't been for Fritz, his constant companion and source of comfort, and his library visits. Danny also suffered greatly from a constant feeling of helplessness. He watched his community being torn apart and could do nothing to help.

All these feelings and events led Danny to become rebellious, which was completely out of character for him. Hans had always been the rebel in the family, while he had always been the compliant one. Danny had often been reminded that one rebel per family was enough. Now, with his new attitude, he was purposely staying out late at night past curfew. The Nazis had started a curfew and everyone had been warned that they had better adhere to it or suffer the consequences. It was intended solely for the Jewish people. However, just to be safe, everyone was encouraged to be inside by 8:00 p.m.

Danny wasn't quite sure what those consequences were, until he himself got caught on his way home by a couple of SS officers after 8:00 pm on a sultry evening late in September. They surrounded him and glared at him, obviously thrilled with his situation. They had been given permission to beat up or even shoot anyone not following the ordinance. Danny was sure he was going to be killed then and there. He could barely breathe; his voice seemed to be trapped in his throat. With every fiber of his being he wanted to stand up to these bastards, who terrorized his neighborhood. But, he knew belligerence would surely have caused these men to torture him, so he opted for subservience. While he hated himself for bowing down to these bastards, he pleaded with them for another chance. He didn't even recognize his own whiney voice. Of all the stupid things he had done in his life, he knew leaving Fritz home that night had been the biggest mistake of them all. At that moment he couldn't even remember why he had.

While he'd been bullied all his life, never before had his life actually been threatened. What would his parents do if they lost their youngest son to these Nazis as well? His whining seemed to only embolden the officers, who proceeded from shoving him around to actually beating him with their fists, and Danny knew it was all over. His glasses were knocked clean off his face and he heard the sickening crunch of glass breaking. At that point Danny knew he wouldn't be needing them anymore. He saw one of them reaching for his pistol and said a silent prayer. He prayed they'd at least shoot him in the head. He had heard that was the least painful way to die, whereas a shot to the chest or abdomen could leave you to suffer for hours before succumbing to the inevitable.

At that moment there arose the most terrifying sound coming from behind him. Everyone froze, not being able to process what they were hearing or seeing. Within the blink of an eye the confidence in the officers' eyes changed to terror. And then Danny knew. There was Fritz by his side with the most menacing growl he had ever heard. Without hesitation, Fritz launched himself at the officer who had just pulled out his gun. With Fritz's humongous size and fury, the officer was no match for a 120 pound dog bent on protecting his master. He was taken down in a heartbeat. Danny could see blood spurting out of a gaping hole in the officer's throat. And within seconds Fritz had taken down the second officer who hadn't had the presence of mind to pull his weapon and shoot this menace. He too shared a similar fate to his comrade, dying almost immediately from his wounds.

Danny looked on in utter horror, though simultaneously he had a strong feeling of triumph at what his dog had done. He had the good sense to get out of there before they were discovered and both killed by other Nazis on patrol. His club foot forgotten in his terror, he literally raced home with Fritz at his heels, keeping an eye out for further dangers. He knew if they were found they were dead. Somehow Danny had had the presence of mind to pick up his broken glasses before they had dashed out of the area.

Once home, in the light of the front porch, Danny noticed all the blood covering both Fritz and himself. He quickly took the garden hose to Fritz and cleaned him up. After he towel dried Fritz, he did his best to clean himself up as well. He couldn't save his bloodied shirt so he threw it in the trash outside so his mutter wouldn't see it.

Finally, shivering under the covers of his bed, Danny knew he couldn't confide in anyone about what had happened. He couldn't tell his parents because he knew it would destroy them.

Danny realized he now had a secret weapon, a fearless companion who could sense danger and would not hesitate to protect him against any threat. How Fritz had found him that fateful night would forever remain a mystery. However, as a result, his love and respect for his dog grew to immense proportions. While knowing it wasn't allowed, he called Fritz onto the bed with him. After that night he was no longer afraid of disobeying his parents. They didn't even notice him anyway.

Finally, from sheer mental and physical exhaustion Danny drifted off to sleep, but not before he came up with a plan. Danny now had a purpose, a goal, a reason to get up each day. With a new determination and courage he never suspected he had, Danny knew what he was going to do. He would be a one man, one dog army. He would train Fritz how to fight silently. He would make a difference. They would be a team bent on murdering every SS officer they could find.

## -16-
## Hans

Training on his new elite squad continued for Hans for another couple of months. While he had thrived at the weapons training, the training they were doing now seemed senseless. They were never given the bigger picture – what were they training for? Hans figured it wasn't likely any of them would find out before it was absolutely necessary. The Nazis were nothing if not furtive, clandestine, and secretive. Yet, in their ignorance, the trainees continued to improve and become stronger and more fit. If any of them showed weakness, their superiors beat them and humiliated them in front of their peers.

The following week, one of the boys finally cracked from the pressure. It was Hans' old friend, Henry. It was early morning and as usual they were expected to get dressed and out of the barracks within five minutes to participate in more endless drills. Henry just sat there on his cot. He appeared to be catatonic. He didn't react when Hans and two of the older boys tried to get him up and warned him about what would happen if he didn't.

Upon hearing some commotion, an SS officer entered the barracks and immediately spotted the cause of the problem. He forced Henry to his feet, only to watch him keel over. When the officer started to kick him and stomp on his hands, Henry just lay there, not even trying to fend off the blows. Not once did he utter a word or even cry out in pain. He was beaten unconscious and finally dragged off by two other guards. He was never seen again by any of his peers. They wanted to believe that Henry just didn't make the cut and was to be sent home in shame. But in their hearts they knew differently. They had already witnessed some of the atrocities these guards had performed.

Strangely, this event seemed to unite the boys in B 17. Perhaps it was the fear that they might be next. Hans, always the natural leader, started having secret talks after lights out. All the trainees, at one time or another shared their stories, their fears, and horror at what they saw daily and what they were being forced to do. They had no delusions of finding a way out of this nightmare, yet it certainly felt better to talk to each other and to promise to have each other's backs. They, like Hans, had figured out that it wouldn't be long before they would be ordered to put all this training to use and would actually have to kill the Nazis' enemies.

It was in late October that they found out the purpose of their "elite" squad. It was a cold, raw day, and without warning, Hans and about a dozen of his comrades were shipped off to Sachsenhausen, one of a network of German Nazi concentration camps built in 1936 in Oranienburg, just 35 km north of Berlin, and 169 km from Hans' hometown of Guben. It was the main training center for SS officers. The camp was roughly triangular in shape and was over a thousand acres in size.

Entering through the main gate, no one could help but notice the huge 8 mm Maxim machine gun over Tower A, where the offices of the camp administration were housed. The camp's commander, Hermann Baranowski, had his offices there.

When Hans and his comrades were brought inside the concentration camp it was as if all the color had left the world. It was a land of greys with no trees or flowers or adornments of any kind. It was all steel and barracks and forbidding barbed wire as far as the eye could see.

The feeling of desolation was palpable. When they saw the prisoners their jaws dropped in utter shock and horror. The boys weren't totally naïve – they knew Jews and Poles had been taken from their homes and brought somewhere, but they had no idea till then the extent of the barbarity. There, they saw thousands of prisoners that looked barely alive. They were skin and bones covered in dirt, scars, and filthy rags. They soon learned that there were several parts to the camp, including forced labor and the death camp. Hans suspected the death camp was probably the most humane of them all. To live in such pain, hunger, fear and filth was unconscionable. At the far western part of Sachsenhausen was the death camp and from just beyond it there rose a continuous disgusting stench. Smoke billowed ceaselessly from chimneys. What they could be burning constantly was beyond Hans' imagination.

The thirteen boys were brought to their new quarters, B 10, where they were accepted without prejudice by the twenty young men who were already there. Somehow they had seemed to have heard what had happened to Henry before Hans and his friends had arrived. Apparently, they also knew about Hans' skill with a rifle, and the recruits hoped he would share his knowledge with them so they, too, could become excellent marksmen. This made Hans feel important and he was more than happy to help.

Hans' immediate superior was Commandant Vogel, who had taken an almost instant dislike to him, and treated him even more harshly than he did all the other trainees. Hans was often forced to do an extra set of push-ups or extra marches in the pouring rain, for no apparent reason other than it seemed to please his leader. The boys all whispered about it late at night. They all suspected it was because Hans was so much better at shooting than anyone else in the camp, an honor that used to belong to Vogel.

"Perhaps he's jealous of your pretty eyes," teased one of Hans' bunk mates. The expected guffaws and comments followed this remark, but none of that bothered Hans.

After several weeks, Hans and two others were given the dubious honor of guarding a large abandoned building. They weren't told what was inside. However, they were warned that if anything went missing they would pay with their lives. The job proved to be fairly easy, since no one would even attempt to get in except several of the SS Elite Guard who were assigned to transport items into the building for safe-keeping. The prisoners could be knocked over with a feather, so weak had they all become. Not once did anyone but the four elite guards try to enter the facility. Yet, Hans and his fellow soldiers were heavily armed and required to stand at attention for endless hours, alert to any possible threat. This was actually a relief from all the punishing physical training they had endured.

Of course, they were all curious as to what was contained therein, but for all, except Hans, the threat of death was enough to curb their natural curiosity. Hans had learned from his brother to be observant. It didn't take more than two weeks before he figured it out. While he would try in vain to peek inside when one guard came to make deposits, the other guards made sure that was impossible by blocking the entrance with their bodies. While he couldn't see through the bags of unknown content or the cloaked pieces, he was able to see the larger items the guards were bringing inside, day after day. They weren't able to hide the bigger objects they brought there; the priceless portraits and small pieces of furniture.

Once, claiming he needed a bathroom break, Hans watched from afar and saw from whence the guards were bringing the treasures. He saw that they were all confiscated from the prisoners when they arrived on the trains that seemed to run all day and night. Danny had been right, again. He had theorized all those months ago that these poor, innocent Jews were told they were being taken somewhere safe and to bring their most prized possessions with them. They were probably advised that they would need them to barter for food and perhaps passage to America. Well, as it turned out, all those valuables immediately became the Fuehrer's treasures.

"What would Danny do?" wondered Hans for the umpteenth time. Danny, his coach, always knew what to do, thought Hans proudly. He used to be jealous of his brother's intelligence, but not anymore. He had learned so much from him and he was determined to find a way to make Danny proud. His grudging respect for his younger brother lost the grudging aspect. He wrote about this in his journal as well, hoping that one day Danny would know how much he looked up to him.

## -17-
## Danny

    Clearly Fritz was already prepared to defend Danny against all threats. However, Danny wanted him to learn to attack only on command and to do it silently, so as not to warn any officers of the impending peril. He also knew he needed to learn all he could about using a Luger and an MP 40 submachine gun, for they would be necessary for him to follow through with his plan.
    Danny once again went to the library and this time he asked Frau Z to help him find books on weapons and on attack dog training. While she was always happy to help Danny out, now that he was looking for these kinds of books, Frau Zimmerman was alarmed. She tried to discuss what this was about, but Danny assured her there was nothing to worry about, it was just his latest interest. Over the years Frau Z had become a trusted friend. And now that his own mama seemed to be living in a different world than he was, he'd gotten even closer to her. She had become a surrogate mutter to Danny. They shared other confidences and loved to talk every time Danny came into the library, which was at least a few times a week. While he ached to confide in her, the one person with whom he actually did consider sharing his secret, he somehow sensed this may endanger her or his planned missions. So he bit his lip and stayed silent. He'd still give her a big smile upon entering and leaving the library. With all his heart he wished he could share his burden. However, he felt he couldn't take that

chance. Eventually Frau Zimmerman stopped trying to pry information from Danny and continued to help him find whatever books he sought, no matter how odd or inappropriate they seemed.

After reading the books, Danny spent every afternoon working with Fritz. Danny was convinced a better pupil didn't exist. It was uncanny how fast Fritz learned and he was always eager to please. Fritz learned "Achtung!" when Danny wanted him to be on guard, and "Fass!" when he was to attack. Danny also knew that he couldn't totally rely on Fritz. He too needed to learn to fight and to somehow obtain a weapon. Could it be possible, he wondered?

That day he took Fritz with him to Chaim's abandoned house. Carefully stepping over the debris, he searched the house from attic to basement. He was about to give up when something caught his eye. Holding his breath he carefully moved broken pieces of wood aside and there underneath was Chaim's air rifle. True, not much of a weapon compared to the rifles and sidearms the officers carried, but he also knew, from a hundred warnings from his mutter, that you could easily take an eye out with it. And, he figured, he'd only need to use the air gun once, effectively. While Danny had somehow had the presence of mind to rescue his broken glasses that fateful night, only one lens was intact. It certainly helped, but he knew he'd have to get pretty close to the SS officers if this was going to work. Nevertheless, this was his strength wasn't it? He'd watch and plan and only make his move when he was confident he would succeed.

After two weeks of breaking curfew to sneak around after dark with Fritz to do reconnaissance, Danny felt it was now or never. He knew where the largest group of SS officers hung out, which was way out of his reach and to be avoided. He had also learned where there would only be two or three officers at the most. He had also been practicing with the air gun for several hours a day in the forsaken field that they had previously used what seemed to be a lifetime ago. He had his doubts if they could take on more than two officers on this first mission, but he was so tired of living in fear. He was so tired of letting these soldiers ruin everyone's lives that he couldn't hide any more. It was past time to take action.

That night he again snuck out with Fritz, the air gun, and with Hans' birthday present, and took up his predetermined spot across the street from where he knew the officers would ultimately show up. To Danny's vast relief there were only two of them that night and they stood smoking under a streetlamp, making them easy targets. He was sure he could hit at least one of them at this distance. He whispered a quiet thanks to his mama for the idea and prayed she was right. Rather than waiting for his common sense and fear to overtake him, he opened fire a second after giving Fritz the command to attack.

Blood gushed from one officer's eye as he screamed in pain and terror. Danny had hit his mark. But, the injured officer wasn't as frightened as his buddy who barely had time to notice a huge black and tan blur lunging for his throat. That one couldn't even get out a scream before he was dead on the ground. Without pausing, Danny ran up to the injured one and whispered, "This is for Chaim's family," right before hitting him in the head with Hans' bat with all his pent up fury and silenced him permanently.

Danny wasn't emotionally prepared for the brutality of his own attack and was at first overwhelmed by what he had done. His head swam and his stomach ached. Nevertheless, he didn't regret his actions. This time instead of immediately running away, Danny, as planned, seized their weapons and then rushed back into the shadows with Fritz. He at least made it out of the area before he had to stop to vomit into the street. Before he could escape to the relative safety of his house, he stashed the weapons at Chaim's house, and quickly did their bathing routine there. As he was hosing Fritz down he realized that some of the blood on Fritz didn't belong to the SS officer – it was coming from Fritz.

Blinded with fear, Danny quickly searched for the wound and found a small two inch puncture wound on Fritz's left shoulder. Fortunately, to Danny's vast relief, it wasn't deep. It was only a flesh wound, and it didn't seem to hurt Fritz at all. After applying pressure for several minutes with some clean bandages from the Schwartz's medicine chest the bleeding was curtailed. Danny didn't know how it had happened, so intent was he on taking out the second officer, yet he was seriously distressed at his best friend's injury.

Shaking with anxiety and stress, but also with a serious sense of accomplishment, Danny finally made it home. He took Fritz into bed with him and lavished love and praise on his partner. They had done it. And they would do it again, and again, as many times as fortune would grant them before he got himself killed. He figured that was inevitable. What disturbed him the most was that he was risking Fritz's life as well and what right did he have to do that? Fritz had been nothing but loyal and the best friend a boy could ever hope for. Fritz had to become his second line of defense. He would not risk Fritz's life unnecessarily again. Danny finally fell into a fitful sleep trying to come up with a way to minimize their risks. He had real weapons now...that would clearly make a difference.

# -18-
# Hans

In November of 1938 when Hans learned that he was going to be transferred from his "cushy" job of guarding the Fuehrer's treasures, he knew he'd have to act very quickly. He was finally going to make Danny proud of him. The plan was in place; all he needed was the opportunity to carry it out. Fortunately, this was presented the night before they moved him to his new job….

************************************

Hans and a dozen of his comrades from the Elite Squad were brought to the death camp. This barracks actually had a name instead of a number, Hans noticed, not that it mattered in the least. He was now quartered in Ziegler Barracks. As in his previous barracks, these young men all looked out for each other as best they could. After several weeks together they actually began to consider themselves a sort of family. They were all still very young and missed their homes desperately.

One night after Hans took the dangerous plunge and confessed how he felt, it was like the flood gates had opened. The recruits spoke openly and honestly with each other, even though doing so could have led to death if there was an informant among them. When confidences were shared after "lights out," Hans learned that they had all come to hate being there and hated what they were being forced to do. Even the most die-hard supporters of the Fuehrer, who had been swayed by all the propaganda the Nazis had spread, now questioned what they had been told at all those school assemblies. They couldn't keep their feelings bottled up forever, and sharing as they did gave them a sense of belonging. It also lent each of them the strength to carry on even when all they really wanted to do was sneak out and go home; a highly unlikely possibility when surrounded by barbed wire fences and heavily armed guards patrolling the camp's borders.

However, Hans noticed that one of his comrades, an older boy named Gunter, never shared in their talks. He had an unreadable expression on his face and Hans' instincts told him that something wasn't right. He tried several times to engage Gunter in conversation, only to be rebuked each time as he told Hans he had nothing to share. Hans discussed this privately with several of his comrades that he felt he could trust and they agreed to take turns keeping an eye on Gunter. Hans had no idea what Gunter's story was, but he gave Hans a nervous feeling in the pit of his stomach that he just couldn't ignore. It turned out to be a prudent move.

The following day when Hans was finishing his breakfast, two of his bunk mates came rushing up to him and told him they needed to speak to him immediately and privately. After going behind an unoccupied building Heinz spoke urgently, "Karl and I saw Gunter approach a senior officer. We couldn't hear everything they said but we think he shared our confidences. We heard Gunter say, "They're all Jew-lovers," and we distinctly heard the officer say he would take care of it and see that Gunter was rewarded for his service.

Karl was anxiously shifting from one foot to the other while Heinz's hands trembled in fear. They all suspected what would happen next. All the recruits in Ziegler Barracks would be severely punished or worse. They were looking to Hans for guidance and Hans knew he had to act fast. He felt responsible for this problem because he was the one who got everyone talking the previous night. Now it seemed he had endangered everyone in Ziegler Barracks.

With knots in his stomach he directed Heinz and Karl to show him which officer had been informed and then he had them go find Peter and Kurt. While keeping the officer under surveillance, Hans waited impatiently for his friends to return and thought about what they had to do.

Once the five of them were finally gathered together he spoke to them as a leader and gave each of them their instructions. There was no choice – they had to take out both the officer and Gunter. He knew that killing the officer would not be difficult as they all hated him already. Killing Gunter was another issue entirely. He had been one of their comrades and was only a little older than Hans. This would be much harder emotionally. Hans knew he had created this mess and therefore he'd have to be the one to do it. Hans also needed to assure himself that Gunter had truly betrayed them. He asked for one volunteer to help him with Gunter and Peter offered immediately.

Hans and Peter followed Gunter, waiting for an opportunity to present itself. When it didn't, Hans had to create his own. He told Peter to rush up to him and inform him there was a prisoner uprising in one of the abandoned buildings and they needed help. Once Peter lured Gunter there, Hans, who had been hiding behind the door, used the butt of his rifle to hit him in the head when he came through the door. Gunter was knocked to the ground, dazed but still conscious.

Hans glared at him, and asked, "Why have you betrayed us? We did you no harm. What's wrong with you?"

"What's wrong with me!?" bristled Gunter, his voice dripping with disdain. "How can you seriously be asking me that? Look around you, you stupid Jew-lover! You're in a Nazi concentration camp or did that escape your notice? We all hate Jews! They are the reason for all that is wrong with our country or haven't you noticed that either?"

Hans was shaking with anger and could barely control his breathing. He felt like he was gasping for air. "What exactly have the Jews done?" he demanded. "Other than what you have been brainwashed to believe, what have you seen a Jew do wrong with your own eyes? We're not the ones who are disillusioned! You are! My best friend was Jewish and he and his family were the kindest, most generous people I've ever known."

Gunter got to his feet and spewed these words at Hans as if they were deadly bullets, "You disgust me! You all sounded like a bunch of girls last night complaining and whining for your mamas. You should be proud to be serving in Hitler's army!"

"Proud! Proud? Are you insane?" Hans sputtered, "I am deeply ashamed of my actions and of being part of this insanity that you seem to believe in. I wish I could go back in time and change everything. I was completely naïve to even consider joining this incomprehensible genocide of innocent people! The Jews have done nothing wrong!!!"

Gunter just glared at him with such hate that Hans involuntarily took a step backwards away from the loathing that emanated from Gunter. Completely forgetting that Peter was even there and thinking he had the advantage, Gunter lunged at Hans only to be hit in the head again, this time with Peter's weapon. This time he was knocked unconscious.

Peter looked at Hans for direction. They both knew they couldn't risk a shot and being discovered, so they concurred that they had to finish the job with a knife. Peter offered to do it and Hans immediately agreed. It alarmed Hans to some degree how easily Peter killed Gunter with the knife, but he was secretly grateful it was Peter who did it. While he had an affinity for guns, knives required too close contact for Hans' liking. Rather than risk being seen dragging Gunter's body elsewhere they just left him there to be discovered eventually.

Meanwhile Heinz, Karl, and Kurt had successfully managed to kill the officer without being seen. They had approached the officer and told him that they heard some of the boys from Ziegler Barracks talking about escaping from the camp. Karl informed him that they had seen these recruits leave their posts and that they were heading west in the direction of the unused, open field on the far side of the death camp. The officer, not knowing these same boys were from Ziegler Barracks, followed them immediately. Once they were out of sight of anyone else and at the designated area, Karl, who had purposely lagged behind, shot him in the back. They disposed of his body under a huge pile of garbage in the rubbish heap close to where they had led him.

That night there was a clandestine meeting in their barracks. Hans told the rest of the recruits what had occurred. They all stared at him wide-eyed in fear for what could have happened, and in awe at how quickly the problem had been solved.

Peter addressed everyone with his concern, "We have no way of knowing if there could be another traitor among us," at which point everyone began to regard each other suspiciously.

Hans spoke clearly and authoritatively, "If there is, be warned that you will be found out and tortured before we kill you." He gave them the gruesome details of the brutal killing of Gunter to make any possible traitor think twice. Then Karl told them how they had disposed of the officer.

Hans warned them, "You are each entitled to your opinions of our situation, but we are all brothers here. Nothing we say in here is to leave these walls. Is that understood?"

All the boys either nodded their agreement or spoke out in support of Hans. Later Hans spoke privately with Peter, Kurt, Heinz, and Karl, the boys he knew he could trust. They all agreed to be vigilant and to keep an eye on their bunk mates.

Nevertheless, things were never the same again in their barracks. There was always a feeling of tension in the air. There were furtive looks and wary stares and a general feeling of unease, which just added greater misery to the already miserable life they were being forced to lead.

\*\*\*\*\*\*\*\*\*\*\*\*\*\*\*\*\*\*\*\*\*\*\*\*\*\*\*\*\*\*\*\*\*\*\*\*\*\*\*\*

It was shortly after this betrayal of their trust that Hans first heard of Kristallnacht from Peter, who had overheard some officers talking about it. Hans learned that a massive, coordinated attack had been launched against Jews throughout the German Reich on the night of November 9, 1938. He heard that 8,000 Jewish homes and businesses had been destroyed and over 30,000 had been arrested. In the immediate aftermath of Kristallnacht the streets were littered with broken glass from the vandalized buildings, giving rise to the name, Kristallnacht, which meant the Night of Broken Glass. The prisoners were being sent to several concentration camps including Sachsenhausen.

The next day the boys of Ziegler Barracks were given their new assignments. They were ordered to report to an old factory building which had been converted into an armory. When Hans arrived, he was shocked to see Commandant Vogel there. Hans had secretly hoped he'd never see his prior commanding officer again until he was ready to put a bullet between his eyes. Hans had envisioned doing just that on many occasions. Vogel was the one who gave the recruits their weapons with 32 bullets every day and told them to bring it back empty. The recruits had no illusions as to what was expected. They were being sent out to kill that many imprisoned Jews and Poles each day. They were told this would "toughen them up." Hans believed that the reason was that after tens of thousands of Jews had been arrested after Kristallnacht, their camp didn't have room to house so many prisoners, so they "needed" to kill them instead. In fact, 6,000 of the Jews arrested were sent to Sachsenhausen to be worked to death or just shot by the new recruits.

On the first day of these new orders, one sympathetic officer whispered to Hans that he should think of it as putting them out of their misery, and that it would get easier over time. He also warned him not to look into their eyes. Having no choice, as Vogel always seemed to be watching him, Hans tried to pick out the feeblest among the prisoners, figuring they wouldn't be long for this world anyway. He convinced himself that wherever they went after this life had to be better than this place. Even Hell had to be better than the life these wretched prisoners somehow endured. It was absolutely amazing how the human spirit had such a strong will to live and how it always carried hope, which gave them the strength to survive daily in the most horrific conditions known to man.

At least half of his barracks, including Hans, were physically ill after they were forced to kill their first prisoner. With all their training, they were unprepared for the amount of blood, brain matter, and Gott knew what else, that spewed from their dead bodies. Even their worst nightmares were nothing compared to actually taking a life. Perhaps if they truly believed, as most of the Nazis did, that these people were really evil, it would have been far easier. Hans could not believe what that officer had told him; he could not imagine this ever getting easier. Most of the boys in Ziegler Bunk cried themselves to sleep that first night horrified at what they had done; others prayed for forgiveness. After writing in his journal, Hans just stared at the wall and promised himself he was going to find a way to get out of there and back to his family. The rebel in him was revived that day and all he wanted was to be as far away from this torture as he could be. He missed his brother, his dog, and his parents, and ached to see their beloved faces again. His mutter used to say, "Where there is a will, there is a way," and with that thought he finally drifted off to sleep.

## -19-
## Danny

Now that Danny had real weapons, he knew he'd have to learn to use them effectively. He knew that firing a real rifle was going to be significantly more difficult than using the air gun. Danny had read that real rifles had a powerful kick to them when fired that often caused the shot to go high and wild.

Though Danny itched to fire the real guns, he knew preparation was important. He knew he had to find a way to get his mama to sew a thick pad into the right shoulder of his jacket without her becoming suspicious. It turned out to be easier than he expected. He made up a story about some bullies who constantly punched him in that spot every chance they got, and this would be an easy way to protect himself from injury. She complied without questioning him, but the look in her eyes told Danny that she doubted his story. At first, he wondered why she abided by this request without an inquisition, but he was too distracted to give it any serious thought.

The next concern that Danny had to address was that he needed to train with these weapons quietly, without calling unwanted attention to himself. While the lot where they used to shoot was vacant and at least a mile away from any residences, he wasn't sure how far the sound of a rifle would carry. To be safe he needed a way to suppress the sound.

As always, when Danny needed to learn something he went to the one place that contained all the information in the world, or at least that was how it appeared to him. However, when he got to the library, Frau Zimmerman was nowhere to be found. Upon asking another librarian with whom he was familiar about her, he learned she was home sick with a cold. He asked if he could have her address so he could visit her. The librarian was hesitant to give out those particulars. After promising he wouldn't tell Frau Zimmerman where he had found out her address, she finally agreed. Since she had seen Danny talking to the Head Librarian on many occasions she didn't think it could hurt. Subsequently, she helped him find the books he sought. Perhaps it was better Frau Z wasn't there that day, Danny thought. While he missed seeing her, he was feeling uncomfortable lately with the wary, knowing look she gave him whenever he asked for books on military tactics. He still longed to confide in her, but was too worried about the possible consequences if he did.

After reading one of the books, Danny was actually amazed at how easy it was to build noise suppressors for the rifle and the pistol he had taken from the dead SS officers. He used two old soda bottles and cut the end off the larger one so the smaller one could fit partway inside. He then adapted it to fit over the end of the weapons and taped it in place so that when the bullet exited the rifle it went through the bottle, which surprisingly deadened the sound of the shot. By doing it this way it was supposed to help hide the source of the shot without interfering with the velocity or accuracy of the bullet.

Danny was thrilled when he was able to use ingenuity to solve a problem. He might not be strong or be able to run fast, but he was going to become a strategic fighter. He would use his brain, rather than have to worry about his brawn, which he knew was seriously lacking. He figured he was as ready as he was going to get as he set out for the abandoned lot with Fritz by his side. He realized that Fritz was going to have to get used to the sound of rifle fire sooner or later, and better to do it gradually using the suppressor so that he didn't spook his dog.

As soon as he began his target practice, Danny realized that his preparations were not in vain. Even with the padding, he could feel the kick of the rifle which he knew would take some getting used to. The suppressor for the rifle worked like a charm, but he noticed that the one for the Luger began to melt after several uses due to the fact that the handgun got hotter when fired than the rifle. He would have to build a better one, preferably out of a metal pipe if he could get his hands on one, or have multiple replacements ready to go. He used his limited ammunition prudently since he wasn't about to go out on any further missions until he was ready, and needed to save enough of the ammo for their next attack.

Fortunately, having previously learned how to adjust for windage and how to elevate or lower his weapon based on other climatic factors, learning how to use his new weapon didn't pose too much of a problem. Using the Luger pistol was a walk in the park compared to using the rifle, and for now that was his weapon of choice, considering that he fully intended to be reasonably close to their next victims. Fritz, being the wonder dog that he was, got used to the noise and quickly picked up on the new commands he had to learn while accompanying Danny on their upcoming missions.

Finally, Danny felt they were as ready as they were going to get. Danny knew he possessed the "home field" advantage. He knew his town better than these SS officers and would be able to move around through alleys and abandoned buildings with ease, virtually unseen. So, after an assault, he was fairly confident he and Fritz could get away quickly and quietly.

When he got home that evening he remembered to ask his mama if she would make a pot of chicken soup to bring to Frau Zimmerman to help her over her cold. Always ready to help out a neighbor, especially one that treated her son so well, Emma was happy to comply. She was even proud of the fact that Danny was being so thoughtful. She knew that he had a special relationship with Frau Zimmerman. Danny promised his mama he would bring it to her the next day, and then hurried off to his room to read his latest books.

Listening to the news that evening, Danny learned of Kristallnacht, the latest atrocity the Nazis had inflicted on the Jewish population. Of course, the propaganda hailed this as a huge victory. Danny was appalled by this increase in violence, and it only fueled his resolve to fight back for all those who couldn't.

## -20-
## Hans

On a frigid January morning in 1939 there was a change to their routine. Hans and a dozen of his colleagues were each ordered to bring ten prisoners to a particular meeting place the next day. Hans couldn't delude himself. He had a fair idea as to what was in store for them. He had overheard one guard talking about giving the recruits a taste of a mass execution. Hans wasn't sure if this was going to be easier or harder than killing prisoners face to face. He had knots in his stomach. He also suspected this was yet another result of Kristallnacht, which had caused the overcrowding in the camp. He knew the Nazis couldn't care less about the living conditions of the prisoners. He suspected it had some kind of negative impact on their bottom line; the costs of running the camp.

The following day there were over a hundred prisoners lined up by what looked like a huge trench, and that's when Hans saw her. She looked awful, barely recognizable, but he knew it was Lilly standing there with all the others. Hans had long ago stopped thinking of her. The awful life he now led didn't lend itself to thinking of girls. For the first few months, he had secretly hoped that he would be trained to patrol his old neighborhood. He dreamed that Lilly would see him in a new light and he would finally have the nerve to talk to her. With all the horrors he had witnessed in the last months, her memory had faded until now. Hans had assumed she was still living in her fancy home. Now he remembered that he had heard that even though Lilly's vater was German, her mutter had been Jewish. That apparently was enough for the Nazis to consider her to be tainted, unclean, the enemy. Even all of her family money couldn't protect her.

Lost in shock and his own private reverie he barely acknowledged the order to open fire. Hans tried in vain to think of this as merciful; better to end their tortured existence and relieve them of the suffering they experienced daily. The majority of the recruits and even the officers couldn't shoot accurately at all. They relied on sheer numbers to take down their enemies. If enough bullets were fired, chances were they would succeed and they usually did.

Yet, Hans couldn't shoot them. He made the mistake of looking into their eyes, which he had been warned not to do, and saw the fear and hope there. It was the hope that tore him apart. Were they hoping for life or death, he wondered. He knew he had to fire with the rest of them, but he made sure not one bullet hit any of the prisoners. The sound of all those rifles firing at once was deafening, and watching all those bodies fall into the waiting trench was chilling.

For some reason this seemed worse than what he had been doing daily for about a month now. The prisoners fell backwards into what turned out to be an open mass grave filled with hundreds and hundreds of bodies. Hans did everything in his power not to throw up. This was by far the most atrocious thing he had witnessed in his young life. He knew Commandant Vogel would be looking for any sign of weakness from him and he wouldn't give him that satisfaction, so he choked down the bile that had risen in his throat.

While Lilly had never actually been part of his life, Hans mourned for her and her family. In his dreams she had been his girlfriend, his one true love. Though he knew logically this had been a fantasy, he couldn't sleep for nights on end after the slaughter. Every time he closed his eyes, he'd see her sweet, innocent face as it used to be in his old life; a life in which he had never truly appreciated all that he had had. With this epiphany, Hans renewed his vow to somehow return to his home and tell his family how much they meant to him.

# -21-
# Danny

In January, Danny and Fritz went out on the first of many missions. It wasn't too different from their first attack using the air gun, but now they were a much more formidable team. It went more smoothly than Danny had anticipated. With the use of surprise and ambush, they easily took out three unsuspecting SS officers. Danny shot two of them and Fritz took out the last one. These officers had also been hanging out smoking, once again under a street lamp. Danny smiled to himself thinking they should have known that smoking can kill you. He was actually pretty shocked when he realized he could keep a sense of humor after what he had done. Believing with all his heart that he was doing the right thing seemed to alleviate the horror of the situation.

Danny wondered how long it would take before the Nazis came to the realization that this was not a safe location. Danny expected to get a lot of mileage out of this form of assault, knowing that the SS officers' false sense of security would be their downfall. The Nazis thought they were invincible and never at risk when roaming the neighborhoods around Danny's residence. So, they were easily taken down by their Righteous League, as Danny secretly called his one man, one dog assault team.

Each successful mission brought in more arms and ammunition which Danny had to hide. He continued to use Chaim's now uninhabited house as a storage facility. He had even gotten so brazen after about eight missions that he stuck around long enough after the attack to search the dead officers for money. Along with all the coins he had been given by Frau Schwartz, he was beginning to accumulate a fair sum of money. About half of it he kept hidden at Chaim's house and the other half he snuck into his mama's savings jar she kept on the window ledge over the sink. She never asked him where the money came from. But, Danny would notice new dog biscuits being purchased as well as better meals being prepared. Again, he wondered about the fact that his mama wasn't interrogating him, like she would in the old days, the good old days before Hans had left them.

Danny and Fritz continued their silent raids almost nightly. It was February and he kept track of how many officers they had killed. It was fifty-seven of the enemy by then. But, that was a drop in the bucket, and Danny feared that it was only a matter of time before they were caught. In March he got his biggest scare to date.

Of course, the Nazis would seek to avenge the murders of their comrades, and it was clear that many of their deaths had been a result of what had to have been a very large animal. They started going through neighborhoods looking for large dogs who could have killed these officers. How hadn't Danny thought that would happen? How had he not foreseen this eventuality? He had been so intent on the one plan, he had been short-sighted not to have expected this. It was only a matter of time before the Nazis started shooting all large dogs. No, he swore, this can't happen. He would protect Fritz with his life. Really though, what could he do? They would probably shoot him first and then his dog.

Fortunately, a stroke of luck and a glimmer of hope appeared. German families tended to be fiercely protective over their dogs, and this proved to be an encumbrance to the Nazis that they had not anticipated. The Nazis were forced to draw the line at turning their fellow Germans against themselves. It was also in March, after a considerable amount of agonizing, that Danny had one of his brainstorms. Propaganda. That could work for him like it did for the Nazis, couldn't it?

Danny set about starting rumors that he had seen packs of ravenous wolves loose in the neighborhood. This was certainly plausible. Everyone knew that wolves lived in the surrounding countryside. Fortunately, the rumors whispered in the appropriate ears took off like wildfire, getting back to the Nazis. So, the propaganda mill could work in reverse. It wasn't long before signs were being posted about the danger of wolves in their town, and the Nazis had to call off their campaign against large dogs.

Over the course of the next few weeks, as Danny read more he learned how to use other military tactics. He realized he would have to change up his routine, as the Nazis would eventually figure out where and how he tended to carry out his attacks. Danny smiled to himself as he learned to adopt the Nazis own methods of "blitzkrieg," or lightning strike, to his advantage. It gave him great pleasure to use their fighting style against them. He would attack swiftly and then disappear almost immediately into the back alleys of the neighborhood that he knew so well.

On subsequent missions he used an old radio he had found at Chaim's house to lure the unsuspecting SS officers to a particular area where he had rigged a trip wire to a grenade he had confiscated on an earlier mission. It was a strange looking device that reminded him of his mutter's potato masher, but was clearly much more deadly. When hearing the hushed voices coming from the radio after curfew, the officers would naturally go and investigate. Danny had installed the trip wire so that the pin of the grenade would be pulled when the officers passed a designated location. The grenade would then explode within four to five seconds.

On his first few trials he snuck in after the explosion to determine its effectiveness. He found that while sometimes the officers were killed outright, others were maimed, but alive. While the view was gruesome, he needed to evaluate if this was a sensible tactic for him to employ. He figured as long as the Nazis were all incapacitated, this was a safe alternative since he could remain at a much safer distance than when he had been shooting them, pretty much at point blank range. The problem, though, was finding more grenades. Danny wondered if he could learn how to make them.

Another device Danny used effectively on several occasions was a type of a snare trap, which was basically comprised of a loop on the ground that, when stepped in, tightened and lifted the unsuspecting officers off the ground to dangle helplessly from a tree. This wasn't his favorite method by any means because they were difficult to rig up and half the time the officers didn't step into the hidden loops. After reading about them in a hunting book, he just had to give it a shot and was actually surprised when it worked. Danny figured the greater his repertoire, the better his chances of success, and he never tired of learning new tactics.

However, after trying the snare trap on one additional occasion, he decided to give it up for good after what transpired. It was way too upsetting for him and he wasn't even sure why.

Danny had set three loops up and was lying in wait when three SS officers walked by. Two stepped in the loops and the other missed it completely as he had been walking a few paces behind his comrades. The two were immediately swept off their feet and were dangling from the branches of a huge pine tree and yelling at the third soldier. They were ordering him to get them down. To Danny's utter surprise the third officer broke out in laughter. He laughed so long and hard that tears were rolling down his face and he was clutching his stomach. At first Danny almost started to laugh as well, as the officer's laughter was so long and loud, it was almost contagious. Danny couldn't help but smile at the sight of those two proud officers hanging upside down and wriggling around helplessly while they shouted obscenities at the officer on the ground for not acting on their orders. Danny could have easily taken out all three of them, but something held him back.

Danny suspected it was the laughter as it seemed to humanize his enemies, which was not a good thing. Danny felt as if he couldn't shoot them in this ridiculous situation. In the past, they had just been nameless evil people who needed to be stopped for all their endless acts of cruelty. This felt different...until the officer on the ground did the unthinkable.

When he finally got control of his laughter and sobered up, he began to circle the officers in the air while talking to them. He addressed his commanding officer in a very disrespectful tone and told him, "I want you to know that I wasn't happy that you promoted your incompetent nephew ahead of me when you knew I was clearly the better candidate for the job." He told the second one, "I am really going to enjoy this revenge for what you did to my best friend. He made a simple error and did not deserve the beating you gave him. It is unlikely he'll ever be able to walk again."

Danny had no idea what the officer was talking about. The man was clearly enjoying his entrapped superiors' predicament immensely. It was when the man took out his side arm and shot them both that Danny was almost too stunned to move. Danny thought he understood war, way better than he had ever wanted to, and felt it was crystal clear. There were your enemies and your allies. You fought your enemies and stood by your friends. The thought of turning on one's comrades was so foreign to him that he was shocked.

Danny was able to pull himself together before the third officer had a chance to leave the area and he took him down with one shot. He no longer appeared to be this jolly stranger having a bit of fun with his colleagues. He was again the personification of pure evil, as all the Nazis have been to Danny.

## -22-
## Hans

In March, while on his mandatory patrol to kill prisoners, Hans heard a faint, but familiar voice call his name, "Hans? Hans is that you?"

Turning around, Hans looked into his old friend's face. He, like Lilly, was barely recognizable. Whereas he had always been chubby and jolly, now he was nothing but flesh hanging off brittle bones.

"Oh mein Gott, Chaim, is that you?!?" Hans sputtered, at once delighted to see his friend and dismayed to see Chaim in this condition. Instinctively he wanted to hug Chaim to him. He wanted to comfort him and save him from this Gott awful place. Hans was ashamed at what his friend saw when he looked at him. What had he become? What kind of a monster did what he was doing???

Yet, all he saw in his friend's eyes was compassion. Hans was taken aback by this. How could Chaim feel compassion for him? How could Chaim know the suffering and torment he experienced daily from what he was being forced to do? How could he understand his pain when Chaim was clearly suffering so much worse? And yet, there it was. He obviously did understand Hans' pain and loss. Hans had always thought of Chaim as one of his best friends, one he had always looked after. And now he swore to himself that he would do it again.

Hans told Chaim, "Don't be afraid. However, for appearances I'm going to pretend to be taking you around the building to be shot." He pointed his gun at Chaim and "forced" him to go behind a deserted building where they could talk in relative privacy and safety. Then Hans asked him what had happened.

Chaim told Hans, "Back on that horrible March day three Nazis showed up on our doorstep while I was downstairs playing with Fritz. I could hear everything they said to my parents. The officers told them that no Jews were allowed to live in our area any longer and that they needed to accompany them to their new living quarters. They informed my parents that resistance was futile. They needed to follow them immediately. Not having a choice my parents left with one of the officers, I imagine at gunpoint. They didn't say a word about me being downstairs, and I had given Fritz the command Danny taught him to stay quiet. But, my parents' efforts to save me were in vain. As soon as they were out of the house the other two officers began to ransack our home, breaking furniture and taking our things. Eventually, they came downstairs and found me hiding behind the sofa, just after I had locked Fritz in the closet and again ordered him to stay quiet, in the hopes that you and Danny would find him. Then they dragged me upstairs and took us on a train to this concentration camp."

Hans hung his head. Clearly Danny had been right, again.

The question in Chaim's eyes was crystal clear.

"Yes, Danny and I found him and took care of him. He is fine. He is with Danny and my parents now." This seemed to provide Chaim with some relief.

"I'm glad you found him. I know you have given him a great home. He always liked you better than me anyway," Chaim tried to smile, but couldn't even seem to muster the strength to do that. "I haven't seen my parents since I got here. We were huddled together after being forced off the train. One of the soldiers tore me out of my mama's arms and I was brought to the work camp. I was able to see my parents board another train that drove in the direction of that place where all the smoke pours from the buildings. I assume that is a work camp for the grown-ups. I keep praying I'll see them again."

Hans didn't have the heart to tell his friend what that place actually was. What was the point? To change the subject he asked, "So how did you get to the death camp if you were in the work camp?"

Chaim explained in a heavy, tired voice, "I got sick and passed out one day and woke up here."

Hans promised Chaim he would do his best to watch out for him. He told him he would tell his fellow comrades he was off limits and he would try to sneak him food every day. This wasn't going to be easy with Vogel, ever present, watching Hans like a hawk, just waiting for him to mess up. For some reason, perhaps there was a Gott after all, Vogel wasn't often around for that month. There was talk of him being trained for another post.

Hans was true to his word, at least he was for three weeks anyway. He kept Chaim alive and brought him as much food as he could smuggle out of the mess hall. The irony wasn't lost on either boy – both remembered how Chaim's kind mutter used to feed Hans – but neither felt the need to bring that up. Often it was his own food he gave up to feed Chaim, which gave Hans a small bit of satisfaction to be helping his friend at his own cost and peril. Chaim wolfed down whatever was brought. He was always ravenous and thanked Hans every time. Chaim was actually starting to look, not healthy by a long shot, but at least further from death than he had when they had first found each other again. Hans encouraged him to stay alive and he promised he would somehow get him out of this hell hole and bring him home. Whether Chaim really believed this was possible, Hans didn't know, but he was determined to find a way. Once again he thought to himself, what would Danny do?

On most visits they talked of old times. They reminisced about shooting Chaim's air rifle and about baseball games. Hans tried to lift Chaim's spirits with anecdotes of what Danny had taught Fritz and how he and his brother would actually vie for Fritz's attention.

"One time we were playing with him by the river. Danny had found an old ball that he was throwing for Fritz. Just for fun, I started to throw sticks for him to fetch as well. We ran him ragged chasing after both the ball and the sticks. Fritz would always bring the ball back to Danny and the stick back to me. He is so smart! Then I guess he got really tired of the game because instead of retrieving, he brought the ball and stick to the water's edge and dropped them in one at a time! After that he looked back at us as if to say, "Enough already!"

This actually made Chaim laugh and that made Hans very happy. It was very rare to hear laughter in a concentration camp, especially coming from one of the prisoners. So, Hans would rack his brain for more funny stories to share to please his friend.

Perhaps Hans had become overconfident with the absence of Commandant Vogel and wasn't as furtive as he should have been. For on one of his "food trips," while he was chatting with Chaim behind the deserted building, he saw Chaim's eyes widen in alarm.

Behind him, Hans heard that hated voice, "Hmmm, and what do we have here? You are fraternizing with the enemy and feeding him no less?! Have you lost your mind?!"

Hans' mind scrambled for an explanation, anything to stop the inevitable from happening. But, his mind went blank. He should have prepared for this eventuality; Danny would have. Yet, he couldn't come up with a plausible explanation, not that one would have helped he suspected. Vogel had it in for him for many months now.

Vogel pulled his Luger from its holster and put it to Hans' head. Not expecting this, Hans was further thrown by this action. When his brain finally decided to start working again he realized this was far worse than he could have imagined. He firmly expected Vogel to kill both of them, most likely Chaim first, forcing Hans to look on helplessly. But, no, this bastard had something worse in store for him.

Sure enough, Vogel, keeping his handgun pressed to the side of Hans' head, ordered Hans to pick up his rifle and then commanded him to shoot Chaim in the face, a face that was still stuffed with bread. Chaim had frozen and stopped chewing the instant he saw the commandant approach. Unwanted, Hans' self-preservation instinct kicked in. If he shot Chaim would he himself live? Although he didn't realize it at this point, he was desperately seeking a way to stay alive and justify what he feared he had to do. He looked into Chaim's beloved face and saw forgiveness in his friend's eyes. He heard Chaim whisper softly, for his ears alone, "It's okay, Hans."

With tears running down his face, Hans pulled the trigger and watched as Chaim's face exploded upon impact. His body toppled to the ground and it was over. He couldn't believe he had done it! How could he be such a coward? He actually now longed for the next shot to be fired to end the pain he couldn't endure another moment.

But, it didn't come. What he heard instead was laughter. No, it couldn't be...yet it was. Vogel actually sounded amused. When Hans finally had the nerve to turn around he saw a hideous sneer on Vogel's already ugly face.

"You want me to shoot you now, don't you," rebuked Vogel. "Naw that would be too good for you. I always knew you were really weak and pathetic. I know that if I leave you alive you will suffer more than if I shoot you now. Of course, I may at any time change my mind on this matter. We shall see."

And with that, Vogel turned on his heel and left Hans to suffer in silence over the loss of his friend, and the knowledge that he, himself, was truly a coward. Why hadn't he thought to shoot Vogel instead? He was sure he could have managed that somehow. Why hadn't he tried?! It was too late now, and all he could do was lie next to Chaim's still body and sob alone and helpless.

# -23-
# Danny

It was on a windy, chilly April night in 1939 when Danny found the answer he had been seeking for months; or rather it found him. What had been constantly weighing on his mind was trying to figure out a way to be more effective in their raids while minimizing the risk to Fritz. Even with all his clever booby traps and subterfuge, he still felt Fritz wasn't safe.

After a particularly gruesome attack on four officers, Danny was once again on his way home when a dark figure stepped out of the shadows. Fritz was already tensed to lunge and Danny drew his weapon.

Just in time he heard a familiar voice say, "Stop! I'm a friend!" and the young man stepped out with his hands raised. It was Hans' friend, Noah. He hadn't seen him in many months. Danny knew he had witnessed their attack on the officers. Would Noah turn them in? Or would he keep their secret?

Noah told Danny, "Trust me, you're going to want to see this," and he gestured for Danny to follow him. Danny's instincts told him that Noah was trustworthy.

Noah had been a good friend to Hans and he had piqued his curiosity, so Danny agreed. Noah had him follow him through back alleys and deserted buildings till they arrived at a large, hidden building in the woods on the outskirts of town. He beckoned them inside and Danny followed with Fritz at his heels. Inside, it was musty and dank, but it was furnished and there were cots with blankets and pillows. There was a kitchen area with a refrigerator and a sink full of dirty dishes. And there were several large tables covered with weapons and uniforms, charts, and maps. At least a dozen other boys were present, who were all staring at Danny and Fritz with great interest. Many Danny recognized, and there were a lot of new faces as well. It looked like the shabbiest form of a military installation imaginable, but a military installation nonetheless.

At the look of shock on Danny's face, Noah actually laughed. He went on to explain that they may look like a band of misfits, but they called themselves, "The Resistance," an underground alliance of Germans who obviously felt the same way as Danny. They were a group intent on doing whatever they could to fight the Nazis from the inside. Apparently, they had been watching Danny, unbeknownst to him, and had admired his courage, his strategies, and his dog. Not one of them would have had the fortitude to do what Danny was doing on his own. They explained they needed him and hoped they could join forces.

Danny had never felt needed. He had never been sought out for any of his abilities. This was so foreign to him he was at a loss for words. He had never experienced anything like it, but he knew that teamwork was, without a doubt, the way to go. With all this new help he wouldn't have to rely on Fritz any longer to attack. He wouldn't need to put him in harm's way again. Fritz would always be his partner, only now he could remain at a much safer distance. Danny felt like a great weight had been lifted from his shoulders.

\*\*\*\*\*\*\*\*\*\*\*\*\*\*\*\*\*\*\*\*\*\*\*\*\*\*\*\*\*\*\*\*\*\*\*\*\*\*

In the coming weeks Danny thrived in this new environment, where his ideas were respected and the other boys actually looked up to him. In a remarkably short time Danny became one of their leaders. His co-leader went by the nickname, Rebel, or Reb for short. Danny had been shocked when he realized that Reb was a girl. He had only seen her at a distance at first and her long, blond hair had been tucked up under her cap. While he had wondered at the fact that Rebel was the smallest "boy" in the alliance and still a leader, he never for a second thought that a girl would be in charge of a fighting group. Danny figured he had learned his lesson in chauvinism and wouldn't make that mistake again. Danny wondered what Reb's real name was, but no one could or would tell him. Once he got to know her, he liked her a lot. Rebel was a year older than Danny and was very brave and fair. She was well respected by all the members of the Resistance for her combat knowledge and her ability to scout out targets without being suspected, simply because she was a girl, and not perceived to be a threat by the Nazis.

Rebel never vied with Danny for control of their alliance. She welcomed Danny and his superior training and skills with open arms. When Danny asked where she had learned to fight and how to use weapons, she smiled and told him, "I was raised with four brothers, who all treated me like one of the "guys." I went everywhere with them. I learned to shoot when I was seven and how to fix a car engine when I was nine. They taught me self-defense, how to build fires, and even how to drive a car – although we kept that last one from our parents."

Danny was duly impressed and asked how she ended up in the alliance. "Well, I didn't exactly end up here...along with two of my brothers we started The Resistance."

When Danny's mouth hung open in surprise, she went on to explain, "My youngest brother was attacked by some SS officers for being out after curfew; somehow it didn't matter that he wasn't a Jew. He survived, but he was maimed for life. My family already secretly hated and condemned the Nazi regime for what they were doing to our Jewish friends and neighbors. However, after Conrad was injured it was the final straw for me. I cried and raged for days and vowed revenge. Finally, my older brothers sat me down and said they had a plan. That was when we created our alliance. We recruited a dozen guys, who in turn enlisted another two dozen. Now our little army is almost 40 strong," she boasted. "We actually have two other encampments, each led by one of my brothers as I lead this one, and we're all committed to destroying the Nazis."

It was Danny's turn and he shared his story from the time he, like her brother, had been caught out after curfew. Also, like her brother, it didn't matter that he wasn't Jewish. Her eyes opened wide and her jaw dropped in awe when he told her how Fritz had saved him. He related how they had formed their own "Righteous League," and how they had succeeded on their missions.

It was Reb's turn to be impressed by all that Danny and Fritz had accomplished on their own.

Rebel told Danny, "We have also been going out on nightly missions to attack the SS officers, but we haven't been as successful as you and Fritz have been."

Danny said, "I'm more than happy to share my knowledge of weapons and tactics with the group to make them more effective."

And Danny was true to his word. He taught the alliance how to use the weapons they had confiscated and how to use booby traps. They knew they would never be a match for a regiment of Nazis and had to learn better ways to take them out a few at a time in blitzkrieg fashion, as Danny had been doing.

Rebel and Danny spent many hours together discussing tactics and dogs. Rebel was in love with Fritz from the get-go and was extremely impressed with what Danny had taught him.

"Hey, you never told me where you got Fritz," Rebel queried one afternoon.

Danny told her his whole story, including what had happened to Chaim's family, as well as what Hans had done. She saw the raw grief in Danny's face when he talked about his brother. She assured him that Hans would realize the error of his decision and find a way home, which is what Danny prayed for every day.

To take his mind off his brother and to cheer him up, Rebel asked Danny, "Do you think you could train a dog just for me?" And naturally, Danny was more than willing.

\*\*\*\*\*\*\*\*\*\*\*\*\*\*\*\*\*\*\*\*\*\*\*\*\*\*\*\*\*\*\*\*\*\*\*\*\*\*

The following day the two of them went off to find a stray that would become Reb's partner, as Fritz was Danny's. It didn't take long for them to find a candidate.

Sadly, as in Chaim's situation, when the Nazis took a family away, they often left behind the family pet who took to the streets in search of food. They found a very skinny, undernourished dog rooting in a garbage dumpster behind Herr Schwartz's grocery store, which had been ransacked after

Kristallnacht. She was a young, female German Shepherd mix, who they guessed was about 7 months old. Her oversized ears gave her a comical, yet enchanting look. Her right ear stood straight up while her left one flopped over. You couldn't help but smile when you looked at her. Her eyes were bright and she looked as if she always had a big grin on her face.

"Maybe she'll grow into her ears," Danny laughed.

"I certainly hope not!" responded Rebel. "I think she is perfect just the way she is!"

Rebel named her Blaze. Blaze was a little shy at first, but took to Fritz immediately. She, like Danny, thought Fritz walked on water, and she was his shadow wherever he went. It didn't take her long to bond with Rebel either. The four of them were rarely seen apart after Blaze was brought back to camp.

Danny and Reb had a blast trying to train Blaze. It was a great relief from going on their nightly missions to be doing something fun and not dangerous for a change. Blaze was a hoot, and Fritz became quite enamored with her. She clearly wasn't the sharpest tool in the shed, however, she wanted to please. When she couldn't figure out what she was supposed to be doing, she'd run in circles around them, typically after stealing a discarded item of clothing such as a hat or a glove, and then roll over looking for a belly rub. She was so funny and adorable, they could only laugh at her antics. On the days when it seemed like she would never learn a particular command, Fritz would eventually "harrumph," or at least that was what his snort sounded like, and would take it upon himself to demonstrate what was expected.

Danny ordered Blaze, "Setzen!" Blaze looked to Fritz for help and watched him sit, so she did the same thing and was thrilled by the praise that was lavished on her. When told to

"Platz!" she lied down immediately after Fritz did, and was rewarded once more by her masters' smiles and Rebel telling her, "Braver hund!"

When Danny instructed her to "Brummen!" Blaze listened to Fritz growl. She tried to emulate him and while it came out sounding more like a sick bullfrog, she was once again thrilled by Danny and Rebel's delight.

And so it went. At these times, Reb would say she saw a light bulb go on over Blaze's head, and she would almost immediately pick up on what she was supposed to do. So, basically it was Fritz who ultimately trained Blaze. Yet it was evident to all that she had very limited potential as a guard dog, unless she could manage to lick an SS officer to death. For Blaze, life was all fun and games. So, Blaze became the Resistance's mascot and constant source of amusement, which had been seriously lacking in their lives.

Realizing the enormous value of having trained dogs to aid them in their missions, Reb tried to convince Danny to take in more strays. Danny told Reb, "I will on one condition. I want to stop using our dogs to attack. Even though they are extremely reliable and effective, I've been searching for months for a way to minimize Fritz's risks while still using his other abilities." He told her how Fritz had gotten injured on their second mission, and he couldn't stop blaming himself for it. Danny insisted that none of them would be attack dogs unless absolutely necessary. He just wanted to use them for their superior sense of hearing to alert them to potential threats.

Reb readily agreed, and so they tried to train other dogs, like Fritz, to fight silently beside them and to only attack on command. The truth was that only two of their new "recruits" proved to be successful at learning those behaviors. It also took a lot longer to train these other dogs than it had to train Fritz, which only confirmed Danny's belief that Fritz truly was a "wonder dog." But, Gretchen and Dash had made the grade and would accompany them on future missions. Dash was young and extremely energetic. He and Blaze played together frequently to everyone's amusement, often chasing each other and rough housing in the fields. Gretchen was an older dog and took to muttering Blaze. When Blaze got into mischief both Gretchen and Fritz would look at each other and Rebel would swear she could hear them both sigh.

After another brainstorm, Danny taught the dogs who didn't take to attack training to guard the perimeter of their camp. Each dog was assigned to one of the members, who would patrol the edges of their encampment as a base defense. This proved to be a lot easier for these dogs to learn. They were taught to fuss and brummen softly when they heard a noise, alerting their masters to any possible danger. While their encampment was pretty well hidden, caution was always a prudent action in these unpredictable times.

An ongoing problem for the alliance was having enough food. As always, what Danny didn't know he learned from books. So Reb and Danny read together and then worked on training the dogs who "failed" attack training and border patrol to retrieve the birds the boys had shot in the fields by the forest, which included ducks, geese, and turkeys. They had already been stealing potatoes, vegetables, and even chickens from nearby farms. They justified it all for their cause. The Resistance had to eat. Using the dogs for so many things proved to be good for all concerned; the dogs had a new home and family, and the Resistance had very helpful, furry friends.

*******************************

When Rebel and Danny were out scouting for supplies in town, Danny felt depressed by all the abandoned homes and shops. The Nazis would no longer allow a Jewish person to own their own business. Glass still crunched underfoot as they walked through the small town. It was very upsetting, but it only served to fortify his resolve to make a difference in his community.

When he shared what he was thinking with Reb, she knew she should try to lighten the mood. So she told Danny, "Would you believe that three of the guys have complained to me this past week about their missing socks!? You'd think they'd have more important things to worry about! They all blame Blaze for stealing them...can you believe that?"

Danny knew it was Blaze without a doubt, and was pretty sure Rebel knew it as well. He responded with a smile, "That's funny you bring it up, because I've lost a couple of pair myself. Let's stop and buy a bunch at Frau Ingrid's shop to replace them all."

Rebel laughed, "That's a good idea. I can't imagine why they would think it was my dog for heaven's sake! I mean I haven't worn a matching pair since we brought Blaze home, but I'm sure that's just pure coincidence."

Danny had come to love being part of this alliance, and Rebel and the dogs were the best part. While he had to admit he would never have dreamed he would actually be killing German soldiers, he believed with all his heart that they were doing the right thing. While in many ways they had become savages, he never considered the Resistance to be bullies because what they did was for a noble cause and that made all the difference. The Resistance became his new family. Very few of the members even went home more than a couple times a week to assure their families they were still alive, and to sneak whatever food they could back to their camp. The death of every Nazi was actually celebrated by this devoted band of warriors, who took guerrilla warfare to a whole new level. They kept a low profile and always attacked in small groups. With experience they learned that three or four members per team was the optimum number to be both covert and effective.

*******************************

After several months the Resistance began to focus on the arts of reconnaissance and sabotage. Killing a handful of SS officers every night wasn't making enough of a difference. After much discussion, and many nights of observation, Reb and Danny led a team out with a new plan in mind. Fritz, Gretchen and Dash accompanied them.

Using their dogs' keen senses to alert them to prospective perils, the alliance was able to follow several unsuspecting officers on their way back to their barracks. There, they waited under the cover of darkness for several hours until they gambled that all the officers had turned in for the night. Silently, in pairs, they crept up to the windows and lit the fuses to the bottles Danny had designed. The bottles were filled with gasoline with a long wick that went out through the opening in the top. As soon as one boy broke the window, the other threw the flaming bottle through it and then they both raced off to a safe distance. The view was spectacular...the entire barracks caught on fire, lighting up the night sky. Any of the Nazis who tried to escape the burning building were shot by other members of the Resistance, who had their rifles trained on the door. It was their most successful mission to date.

They weren't really sure, but calculated that they had killed at least twenty enemies with that one strike. After doing this at three additional sites, the Resistance wanted to up their game once again and find the Nazi headquarters and figure out a way to blow it up, along with any munitions they had in storage.

**\*\*\*\*\*\*\*\*\*\*\*\*\*\*\*\*\*\*\*\*\*\*\*\*\*\*\*\*\*\*\*\*\*\*\*\*\*\*\***

This endeavor took a lot of preparation. While scouting teams were doing reconnaissance to locate munitions store houses and the Nazis' headquarters, Danny and Rebel were learning how to make home-made grenades. Danny remembered the design from having confiscated a few in the past. Together, they assembled tin cans containing shrapnel on the end of pipes, to which they attached fuses as well as a detonator. Getting the appropriate supplies no longer posed a problem. Either their contacts from the neighborhoods provided what was needed or Danny took pipes out of Chaim's old house. Every time he took something from there to help their efforts gave him a sense that Chaim was helping avenge his family's disappearance, and presumed deaths.

They had to field test the grenades in a safe location before actually going out on their next mission. This subsequently proved to be another victory when they all exploded as planned. All this took several weeks, but as Danny had learned, preparation was the key to every successful mission.

When they were ready, Reb and Danny each led a separate team. Reb's team took on the headquarters, while Danny's larger team attacked the Nazis' ammunition bunkers.

Once his team was in place Danny decided to take a calculated risk, which he hadn't shared with Rebel. Rather than blow everything up, he figured, why not see if they could steal some of the gunpowder to make their own ammo. He quickly reorganized the attack and had his team ready while he and Noah, along with Fritz and Gretchen, crept up to the ammunition depot. They didn't know what to expect and weren't sure how the gunpowder would be stored. There appeared to be only two officers guarding the supply. While Danny hated to do it, he knew their only option would be to send the dogs in to take them out, as firing their weapons would alert too many others to their mission prematurely. He uttered a silent prayer under his breath and sent the dogs in, commanding them to, "Suche! Fass!" They had been trained well and took the guards out quickly and silently. When they returned, covered in the officers' blood, Danny was relieved that part was over, and thanked Gott the dogs weren't injured. Then he and Noah entered the depot and were disappointed to see that the kegs that housed the gunpowder would be too cumbersome to carry.

As it had in the past, ingenuity struck Danny and he directed Noah on how to make a makeshift kind of sled from the wooden crates that surrounded them. They maneuvered a barrel onto it and tied rope to the runners, while the dogs stood watch. It was awkward at best, but they managed to get it out with Danny pulling and Noah pushing.

When the team thought Danny and Noah were in the clear they launched their home-made grenades into the weapons depot. The explosions could be heard for miles. The alliance wasn't prepared for the force of the concussive blast from the eruptions and many of them were literally blown off their feet. The blaze lit up the night sky for hours as all the highly flammable contents burned.

Just as Noah was diving for cover a flaming piece of shrapnel hit him in the leg. He yelled in pain and rolled in the dirt trying to put out the flames. Danny was there in seconds and put the fire out and quickly dressed the gaping wound in Noah's thigh, having learned basic first aid from his mutter. Fortunately, the rest of Danny's team were able to escape in the ensuing chaos, with only minor cuts and burns, and return to camp. Rebel's team was already there, clearly triumphant from their own mission. Two of her men had experienced temporary loss of hearing from the explosions, but were already recovering. The celebration stopped when they saw what had happened to Noah. His wound was grievous, and he was clearly in serious pain.

Danny took Rebel aside and told her about how he had improvised, and how that had resulted in Noah getting hurt. He said it was all his fault. He rambled on and on about how he should have known better and that he should have stuck to the plan, clearly beating himself up over Noah's injury. He was also upset with himself for putting Fritz in jeopardy again, which he hadn't wanted to do. But, the potential to bring gunpowder back to camp was irresistible at the time.

Rebel tried to comfort him, "Danny, stop. This wasn't your fault. The plan may have been improvised but it was a good one. I'd have done it myself if I was as clever as you. The gun powder you managed to steal will help us immensely." This did little to ease Danny's guilt. She told him, "Everyone knows the risks, and this was a bad accident. We can't always come away from what we're doing unscathed. I think you need to talk to Noah and tell him how awful you feel."

Dreading it, but knowing it was good advice, Danny waited until later that night to approach him. Noah's wound had been treated with alcohol and a solution to fight off infection and he seemed to be resting peacefully. Danny apologized profusely and begged Noah's forgiveness.

"There's nothing to forgive, Danny," Noah responded. "This wasn't your fault. And if I didn't think it was a good plan I would have said something. I don't blame you and you need to stop blaming yourself. It will do no good and will keep you from future brilliant plans. I'll be able to walk normally again in about a week. If it makes you feel any better, you could wait on me hand and foot till then," Noah grinned.

Feeling immensely relieved, Danny willingly agreed to be at Noah's beck and call as long as he needed. They spent the rest of the evening discussing the raid and how remarkable their dogs were.

\*\*\*\*\*\*\*\*\*\*\*\*\*\*\*\*\*\*\*\*\*\*\*\*\*\*\*\*\*\*\*\*\*\*\*\*\*

That experience really sobered Danny up. It had felt like they were invincible till then. To make matters worse, the following day Danny got the scare of his life. He and Rebel needed to go back to town for assorted supplies and they decided to split up to save time. They agreed to a meeting spot at the outskirts of their campgrounds.

After completing his errands and returning to their meeting area, Rebel was nowhere to be found, and Fritz began acting very strangely. His ruff was up, his teeth were bared and he was whining softly. This was enough for Danny to pull out his rifle and drop to the ground. He knew better than to ever doubt Fritz.

It was then that Danny saw an SS officer come out from behind some trees with his Luger pressed against Rebel's temple. He wasn't sure if he was more shocked to see an officer so close to their hideout or that one of them could have gotten the drop on Reb.

At this distance he didn't think he could see well enough to shoot the officer without endangering Rebel. Fritz was ready to fly to her defense, but Danny quickly ordered him to stand down as he wasn't confident that he could get there before the officer shot either Reb or Fritz. He was at a loss as to how to handle the situation and his mind was scrambling frantically for a solution. The officer had spotted him and ordered him to drop his weapon or he would shoot the girl. Danny complied and prayed that one of their colleagues would be patrolling the perimeter of their encampment and come to their rescue. What followed was a huge shock to everyone there.

Afterwards she could only be described as a blur...Blaze was so fast that it boggled their minds. She seemed to come out of nowhere and launched herself full tilt at the back of the unsuspecting officer and sent him sprawling onto the ground. His weapon went flying out of his hand from the impact, at which point Danny shot the incapacitated officer. Danny rushed to Rebel and embraced her as she trembled in his arms for several minutes before pulling herself together. Then she turned to Blaze and hugged and kissed her and told her she would buy her all the socks in the world as a reward. She lavished praise on her and even Fritz licked Blaze's face all over. Blaze just seemed to smile and soak it all up. It seemed as if she knew she had finally earned her keep.

After disposing of the officer's body, the four of them went back to camp and called a meeting. They shared with everyone what had happened and everyone celebrated Blaze's achievement. Danny looked at Rebel, who seemed to have recovered completely, and whispered, "I bet no one will be complaining about missing socks again!"

Rebel smiled from ear to ear and replied, "They had better not!"

*****************************

In spite of all the violence and bloodshed, Danny was actually enjoying his life and role in the alliance. While he missed his brother terribly, he felt he found a brotherhood here with these other boys. He was especially thrilled to have found such a good friend in Rebel. He had always tagged along with Hans and had never had a really good friend of his own. Most importantly though, he no longer felt helpless. He felt as if they were doing the right thing and making a difference. They were even beating the odds with all their successful missions. Apparently, brains before brawn really worked!

However, the benefit of brawn couldn't be overlooked, so on Danny's advice the alliance members began to train to become physically strong. They worked out daily and it became a friendly competition to see who could do the most pushups or who could best who at mock hand to hand combat. Eventually they became an even more powerful team.

They knew that they were driving the Nazis insane by their constant, unpredictable assaults. They killed innumerable Nazis and stole so many weapons over the ensuing months that they had built up an impressive arsenal. What they needed now was to recruit more men, which didn't prove to be as difficult as they expected. They had to be discreet; one word about their organization in the wrong ear could bring their alliance to a dead halt, literally.

Fortunately, the members knew who they could trust, who felt the same way as they did about the Nazi regime. They succeeded in recruiting another ten members, and also enlisted the aid of many who wouldn't fight, but who were willing to provide miscellaneous supplies.

Meanwhile, Danny found that by wearing a huge pair of army boots they had confiscated and stuffing them with socks, he could almost walk without a limp. Under Reb's leadership the alliance had then targeted several officers who wore glasses until Danny found a pair that fit and which improved his vision tremendously.

Now that Danny could see greater distances they would take their target practice to a new level. They would train to shoot from a further, safer range, and learn to take out targets in succession. This would be vital where they would soon be going. There would be a much greater number of Nazis on patrol that would need to be brought down swiftly, giving the alliance members a chance to escape before they were overwhelmed by additional troops. They knew they would never be a match for a regiment of Nazis in a normal fight, and they would have to continue to rely on their guerilla warfare training. Danny and Rebel had formed a very aggressive, bold plan and Danny was extremely anxious to see it through.

## -24-
## Hans

Hans was tortured by what he had done. Every night without fail he relived the nightmare. Even writing in his journal provided no relief from the pain he felt. He couldn't forget the look in Chaim's eyes and the undeserved forgiveness on his lips. Hans had taken a life…not just any life…but that of a true friend. What had he become? He couldn't eat or sleep. Hans became weak. Nevertheless, he vowed revenge. All he could do was think and plot. In his journal he made a silent pledge to his Coach that he would find a way and prayed for guidance.

As he agonized and plotted, Hans somehow knew it would be the Nazis' precision and blind need to follow protocol that would bring them down. In fact, Hans decided, Chaim would help him avenge his own death. Chaim would give him the strength to see this through.

Hans finally came to the realization that if he was to succeed, he would need every ounce of strength and courage he could muster. So he forced food down, without even tasting it, and he worked harder than ever at his training. He would become a fighting machine. And with that thought Hans planned his revenge and his escape.

Hans had seen maps of the surrounding area in the Commandant's headquarters when he had been called in one day for disciplinary action, which included a beating, for not following orders. He began to watch the building every night to determine when it was vacant. Finally, when he saw Commandant Vogel leave for dinner one evening the following week he snuck in and stole the maps, stuffing them down his pants. While in a hurry to leave the office before he was caught, he couldn't help stopping by the bookcase that was on the side of the door. Danny had always figured everything out by reading, so he quickly scanned the titles and one caught his eye. "Perfect!" Hans thought. It was a survival manual. He quickly stuffed that under his jacket and crept out of the building. He studied his treasures when he got to a deserted field in an unused part of the camp he had recently discovered. It was here that he learned how to read the maps so he would know where to go once he escaped this Gott forsaken place. And it was here that he taught himself about survival methods.

Survival training now consumed his every waking moment. With a pair of wire cutters he had also stolen, he cut a hole in the barbed wire fence just large enough for him to squeeze through, covering it with brush to conceal it. Recognizing the dangers that lay on the other side of that fence, he nevertheless began reconnaissance of the surrounding areas. He half expected to be caught by one of the countless Nazi patrols, but somehow luck was with him. Perhaps since it had abandoned him for so long, he pondered, luck had found its way back to him. Hans humored himself by thinking he had been very well trained by the Nazis and now he was putting some of that training to good use, not for the Nazis as intended, but for his own purposes.

Hans taught himself how to find water in the woods, what berries and nuts were edible and which were poisonous. He knew he'd have at least a four day hike back to Guben. Having previously been taught how to conceal himself using camouflage, he now lay for hours in the forest unnoticed and figured out the timing of the Nazi patrols that covered this area. As Hans had predicted, the Nazis were nothing if not precise, so it was easy to determine their schedule which was essential for his plan to succeed.

Commandant Vogel was called to another duty for several weeks and this gave Hans the break he needed. Left unsupervised Hans could finally carry out his plan, without having to constantly be looking over his shoulder for his superior.

In the field Hans began to do what he had done what seemed like a lifetime ago with Danny and Chaim. He practiced his target shooting. He spent his 32 rounds each day here, as well as many more. Hans had easy access to virtually an unlimited supply of ammunition. He knew he didn't really need the practice to take out a single target at any range. He needed to learn how to take out five targets in succession quickly, effectively, and without hesitation. Hans knew that even the slightest hesitation would probably lead to his own death.

And so it was that both Danny and Hans began their new rifle training in earnest, teaching themselves to shoot to kill with one shot, and to be able to move on to a second and third target in rapid succession without pausing. Unknowingly, they shared a common goal; to take out as many Nazis as they possibly could. Of course, neither one knew of each other's fate.

## -25-
## Danny

Leaving Reb to supervise the Resistance with their target training, Danny headed off to the library again for additional literature on military tactics. But, when he turned the corner, instead of seeing his beloved library, there was only an immense pile of smoldering rubble. The huge wood and stone building, his safe haven, had been burned to the ground. Amidst the smoke he could barely make out a lone figure, standing motionless, staring at the devastation while small flames still licked at her feet. Of course, it was Frau Z. She stood as still as a stone with tears streaming down her face, which Danny knew weren't a result of the smoke in her eyes. He too felt his chest grow tight and he used all his willpower not to cry as well. He walked up to her slowly so he wouldn't frighten her and gently took her hand in his. At first she seemed oblivious, then she turned to him and pulled him into her strong arms. After several moments in this embrace, she sighed deeply and seemed ready to tell him what had happened.

Trembling with rage and sorrow, her voice dripping with disdain, Frau Z denounced their Fuehrer. She advised Danny that, "Hitler wants to control what everyone reads and the Nazis are involved in a campaign to destroy any literature that they consider to be subversive or that represents opposing ideologies. Sometimes in their zeal, they find it more efficient to just burn entire libraries to the ground, rather than pour over the books. Their goal is to teach blind obedience to the Fuehrer and to discourage independent thinking which they consider to be a dangerous thing."

They stood in silence for several minutes while Danny tried to grasp this new insanity. Then Frau Z told Danny, "There is a bit of good news though." Danny couldn't imagine what that could be and looked at her hopefully. She lowered her voice and in a whisper told him, "I've anticipated this for several months and so I have been covertly saving as many books as I could. I have them stockpiled in my residence." She assured Danny, "I made sure to save the types of books in which you have shown an interest."

Gently, Danny put his arm around Frau Z and guided her towards her home. She seemed to have pulled herself together by then and served tea and pastries she had made the day before. They sat and talked for hours, while going through books she thought Danny could use. Of special interest was a book by a famous Chinese military leader, named Sun Tzu, called <u>The Art of War</u>. It was then that Frau Zimmerman shared her secret with Danny.

Frau Z proclaimed her deep hatred for the Nazi regime, a hatred that existed long before they destroyed her precious library. She explained that while she was German, her husband had been a Jew. "Eighteen months ago my Murray never came home from work and I have no doubt what happened," she divulged. "For some time now I've suspected that you and I were of like mind about the Nazis," she continued, presenting Danny with the opportunity to confide in her...and he finally did.

It actually felt good to be able to talk to someone intelligent, outside the Resistance, who understood what he was doing and actually admired him for it.

"I think you're very brave, Danny. I've suspected for some time that you were involved in some form of resistance movement based on the books you were taking out. I've been praying for you nightly, hoping you weren't taking too many risks."

Danny was glad he could be open with Frau Z. He had longed to tell her on countless occasions. However, he was astonished when she offered to help.

"Is there any way I can be of assistance to your alliance, Danny? It would mean a lot to me to be able to help your noble cause if I could." Frau Z offered.

Danny thought about it for a while and then smiled and inquired, "You are obviously not going to be shooting the Nazis along with us, but are you by any chance a good cook?"

Danny explained that feeding all the soldiers in their alliance was difficult and took time away from more important endeavors. At this, a huge smile covered her face and she said, "I'd be honored to cook for you!" She grinned and added, "Since I'm clearly out of a job, I will need something constructive to do anyway."

With that, Frau Z led Danny down to her cellar where her husband had stocked what seemed like endless shelves of every kind of non-perishable item you could think of...just in case something happened to him. There was even a huge freezer with a large variety of meats and cheeses. Apparently, money hadn't been in short supply for the Zimmermans.

Frau Z smiled at the look on Danny's face, "Can you believe all this food? I thought my Murray was a little crazy when he started to stockpile food, but he always knew what was best. I trusted his judgment, whether I agreed with him or not. It is undoubtedly more food than I could eat for the rest of my life, so I am clearly well prepared to assist the Resistance."

They spent at least another hour discussing a plan for her to deliver the food to them without being seen. They hugged each other tightly before he left, each feeling their bond grow only stronger now that they had shared their secrets.

While still upset about the loss of the library, Danny returned to the Resistance with about half a dozen books and wonderful news. While thrilled at the prospect of hot food, the other members of the alliance were at first alarmed to hear that he had confided in someone outside of their group. Danny assured them that he trusted Frau Zimmerman with his life. At this, there were happy faces all around and they called for a celebration. They spent the rest of the evening eating and drinking without having to worry about running out of their limited supplies. They discussed how not having to steal and sneak food from their homes freed them up for further training and missions.

Danny then brought up an idea that got everyone's attention. He explained, "I want all of you to learn some essential life saving techniques and basic first aid. We have been lucky till now and haven't had any serious casualties. However, I expect it is only a matter of time and luck before some of us require medical attention. There is no way we could, in that event, go to a hospital. A gunshot wound would arouse too much suspicion and could endanger our alliance." Everyone there knew the risks and no one had forgotten what had happened to Noah.

Now that Danny had suggested this, it seemed like only common sense to do it. While Danny soaked up the praise for another brilliant suggestion, he couldn't take credit for this one. He admitted, "It was actually Frau Zimmerman who proposed this idea and provided me with the appropriate books." Danny informed them, "While I want all of you to have basic medical training, I want the soldiers who are not adept at shooting to become the most knowledgeable." He added that one of these "medics" would accompany every single raid in the future. As with all his previous ideas and insights, the rest of the Resistance readily agreed.

Danny was able to purchase the necessary medical supplies with the money he had secreted away.

The timing of this endeavor couldn't have been more fortuitous. For the following week their "lucky" streak came to an end when Emil, one of the newer members of the Resistance, got shot. While Danny and three other members were out on one of their standard missions, one of the SS soldiers was able to get a shot off before Danny took him out. Emil was hit in the calf and was bleeding profusely. He was lucky it was a through and through shot. Fortunately, they had learned enough to pour alcohol onto the open wound and wrap it tightly with bandages to control the bleeding. Danny knew from his studies that this would buy them time, maybe an hour or two, but that Emil would need stitches if he was ever going to walk again.

Danny couldn't believe he was even considering it. Before he could change his mind he directed his colleagues to help Emil get up and to assist him to walk about five blocks. Although one of the youngest of their team, Emil was a tough kind. Though he wanted to scream from the pain, he was determined to keep quiet. He was smart enough to understand that calling attention to themselves would only make matters worse. When asked where they were headed, Danny ignored the question and kept walking.

Fortunately, his vater was out for one of his nightly walks. Danny instructed them to take Emil, who was already light headed from loss of blood, to the backyard and to wait for him there. When he entered the house he found his mama in the kitchen. When she saw the blood covering the front of Danny's sweatshirt she about fell off her stool and cried in alarm. Danny hadn't even realized he was covered in blood. He quickly assured her it wasn't his blood and that he was fine, but that one of his friends had been badly injured. With all the powers of persuasion he possessed he convinced her to sew up Emil's wound, something the Resistance had not yet learned how to do.

Danny had the needed supplies and his mutter had the necessary skill. It wasn't that much different from the sewing she had done all her life. Without asking too many questions, she proceeded to suture Emil's leg after they had iced it to control the bleeding and relieve some of the agony. They had also given him some whiskey for the pain, as well as a wooden spoon on which to bite, knowing that he could bite through his own tongue if they didn't. Looking Danny in the eye, Emma instructed them all to watch closely so that they could do this themselves in the future. Danny got the message. His mutter had suspected for some time what Danny had been doing all the evenings he was out past curfew and the nights when he didn't come home at all. He wasn't quite sure how she felt about what he did, but she had made it clear that she wanted no further part in it.

Before they left for the perilous journey back to their camp, Frau Wolf pulled Danny aside and urgently whispered, "You don't have to be doing this!"

Danny looked her in the eyes and replied, "Yes, Mama, I do."

His mama hugged him tightly and reassured him she wouldn't tell his papa. After helping them to build a make-shift stretcher on which to carry Emil, out of two long poles and some old material Emma had from sewing, Emma hurried them on their way. She had a lot of cleaning up to do before Jacob got home.

## -26-
## Hans

Hans' opportunities to sneak out to the field ended when Commandant Vogel returned to his prior position of handing out their rifles each morning. While Hans acknowledged that his plan wasn't ready, and might never be ready, it was now or never. Would he have the courage to see it through, he worried. Of course he would, he assured himself; after all, hadn't his parents always said he had the heart of a lion?

In December, two weeks before Christmas, Hans woke up and knew this was the day. Hey, he kidded himself, if all went well he might be home for Christmas. Hans knew it wasn't likely that all would go well, yet it was a beautiful thought.

It took every ounce of will power Hans possessed to keep his breathing normal as he entered the ammunition facility at the end of the day to turn his rifle over to Vogel for inspection. He certainly didn't want to call attention to himself before it was absolutely necessary. And if he gave his gun to Vogel, his commanding officer would demand to know why the rifle was still loaded.

So, when it was his turn, instead of handing his rifle to Vogel, he lifted it in one smooth motion and right before shooting Vogel in the face, he whispered, "This is for Chaim." Without pausing for the satisfaction that provided, he turned swiftly and took out the other four armed officers who had stood in the exact same spots every time the recruits came back with their empty rifles. As he had predicted, their blind need to follow protocol proved to be their downfall. Hans knew exactly where each guard would be standing and he had practiced this exact scenario over and over again in that abandoned field. However, the last officer Hans turned to shoot got a couple of shots off before being hit. One went wide and one grazed the side of Hans' shoulder. While by no means a mortal wound, the pain seared through him. He forced himself to ignore it.

Hans wasn't prepared to be a hero. He had no thought for the rest of his comrades. Through all the shouts and encouragement of his peers, he had only one goal now…to get out alive…to make it home to his family…to apologize for what he had done. He was under no illusion he would survive – he knew they would hunt him down. He also knew there were many SS officers patrolling outside the barbed wire fence. Hans knew he had to try. He couldn't live with himself if he didn't.

Running on adrenaline, Hans somehow managed to get himself out of the facility in all the commotion that ensued. He made it back to the deserted lot and crawled through the barbed wire fence where he had previously cut out a section in preparation for that night. And he ran. He had no idea how long he ran or how far he had gotten. He just knew the general direction he needed to go and the adrenaline and distant hope of seeing his family again kept his legs pumping. His SS training was finally coming in handy.

# -27-
# Danny

Danny and his comrades had become very successful at guerilla warfare. They worked as a well-oiled machine by December. They actually lost count of how many Nazis they had eliminated, without one casualty and only two serious injuries on their side.

The Resistance's next bold plan was to take the fight to the Nazis' home territory rather than continue with their cloak and dagger techniques in their neighborhood and surrounding areas. The team knew their next challenge would be much harder than anything they had done before. The borders of the concentration camps were heavily guarded, and that, of course, was their destination.

Their first stop would be the closest camp to Guben, which was Sachsenhausen. It was approximately 170 km away. They needed to acquire two vehicles to get them there. Reb already knew how to drive and knew she would be able to use her family's car for this brave endeavor. Her family supported the alliance in any way they could. However, the second car needed to carry Danny's team was a problem. One of the older boys, Alexander, knew how to drive, but didn't have a way to get a car. Danny's family had been too impoverished to own one. His poor papa had always had to walk three miles to and from work daily. After much discussion, Danny agreed to ask if they could use Frau Z's car. She was already doing so much to help them that Danny didn't really want to ask for more. A car was essential and short of stealing one, they didn't have a choice. While their goal was to kill the Nazis, they couldn't bring themselves to take from their fellow countrymen, who they had sworn to protect.

When Danny visited Frau Z and told her of their plans and what they needed, she agreed without hesitation. She told Danny that she hardly even used it any more. It was her husband who used to drive it.

"You can have the car, Danny, no problem. But are you sure you know what you're getting yourself into? What you're planning is going to be way more dangerous than anything you've done before."

"We know," Danny responded, "but we believe this is the only logical course of action at this point. We're even hoping ultimately to free some of the prisoners. We don't have much intelligence on the concentration camps, so this will help us scope it out. Don't worry, we'll be taking extra precautions."

It wasn't necessary for Danny to spell it out. Frau Z knew what Danny was actually hoping to accomplish. It was a chance in a million, but she knew he had to try. He had never given up on his brother and she admired Danny even more as a result. Without another word she handed Danny a picture of her husband. Words weren't necessary; Danny knew what she was asking him. He put the picture in his pocket and told her he would do his best.

It took another week before all the arrangements were made and the alliance was on their way. Once at the outskirts of the concentration camp, they set up their carefully concealed encampment in the woods and again went over their plan in detail.

The teams were planning on using their latest strategy, which had proved to be very effective. Danny and Reb had designed several large camouflaged tarps, under which six Resistance fighters could hide. After careful observation they would learn the Nazi's patrol schedules. As an unsuspecting patrol passed within a few yards of them, they would remain hidden until the last footsteps had passed. At that point they would pull the tarp off in one swift, practiced move and assault the Nazis from behind. This would give them the element of surprise and also hopefully give them the extra time they needed to shoot several times before the confused patrol realized what was happening. Well, that was the plan anyway. Time would tell if it would work.

It was the middle of December and they planned on continuing till Christmas, at which time they would take a much needed break and return to their families for a couple of weeks before resuming their endeavors. Danny and Rebel had even made some plans to do something fun for a change during the break.

As usual, Danny and Reb each led separate teams to improve their odds and to hopefully increase the damage they intended to inflict on their last missions of the year.

After a few days the two teams met up and shared what they had learned and what they had achieved. Apparently, Reb's team had been way more successful in taking down a greater number of SS patrols, though Danny's results weren't too shabby either. Reb reported that one of her team had been injured and they were going to head back early. Danny told her that they would carry out one more attack that night and then would meet her back at camp.

\*\*\*\*\*\*\*\*\*\*\*\*\*\*\*\*\*\*\*\*\*\*\*\*\*\*\*\*\*\*\*\*\*\*\*\*\*\*

Right outside of Sachsenhausen, Danny, Noah, Frank, and their medic, Alexander, were being especially cautious. This area was covered with Nazi soldiers, and they knew they couldn't let their guard down for a second. Danny always kept one eye on Fritz though, because when Fritz's ears perked up, that was their signal to drop silently to the ground and take aim, all rifles pointed in the direction that Fritz was facing.

But, for the first time ever, Fritz broke protocol. A long, low whine emanated from his chest, and his tail began to wag furiously. Danny had never seen or heard him do anything like this...there had to be a reason...he trusted his dog more than he ever trusted another human being. The Resistance took their positions in a heartbeat with rifles raised in a swift practiced move. However, before Danny had the presence of mind to order his comrades to stand down, their shots rang out when they saw an SS uniform emerge from a cluster of trees...and one of those shots found its mark.

Fritz whined and pulled so hard at his lead Danny couldn't hold him. He could do nothing to stop Fritz from flying towards the soldier as the bullets rang out. And then he saw the unthinkable.

The soldier went down and Fritz was all over him, licking him and crying piteously. It can't be, thought Danny, it can't be. He ordered his men to stand down and rushed over to the fallen officer and looked down into the most beautiful eyes he had ever seen.

Secretly he had always admired those eyes, though he had never told his brother, out of jealousy no doubt. He had figured since everyone else seemed to tell him how special his eyes were, he hadn't felt inclined to add to Hans' already swollen ego.

"Ach du grofser Gott! Ogottogottogott! What have we done?!" Danny swore as panic overcame him. Not waiting for his medic to appear with the needed bandages, he quickly tore off his own shirt and stuffed it into the bullet hole in his brother's side to staunch the bleeding.

Sobbing, Danny's words came out in a rush, "Hans I'm here now, you've got to hold on. I will get you to safety. It will all be ok. I have friends with me. We've formed a resistance movement and we can save you!"

But, Hans knew better. A strange calm had overcome him. He felt blessed to see his beloved brother one more time. Hans clasped his brother's hand in his and admitted that Danny had been right all along.

Hans confessed, "Danny I've been so blind, stupid and naïve and you, as always, were right. I'm so sorry...please forgive me. I should have listened to my Coach." Hearing this melted Danny's heart.

Hans continued to beg for Danny's forgiveness as he hugged Fritz to him and cried for all that he had lost and all the pain he had caused his family.

Danny assured Hans, "Of course you are forgiven! You're my brother and I love you with all my heart! You have no idea how much I've missed you! I have so much to tell you!"

With a squeeze of Danny's hand, Hans communicated to Danny that he needed him to stop talking and listen. Hans knew time was precious and he needed to tell Danny some important things before it was too late. First, he made Danny promise not to tell their parents how he had died and to please make him out to be a hero, who had learned too late that what they had been trying to tell him all along was the truth. At least, Hans continued in barely a whisper, he had learned, and now he would save them all. He told Danny that he had found a way to get their family to America, to safety.

Danny couldn't understand what Hans was talking about and assumed he was getting delirious from the loss of blood. Nevertheless, when Hans told Danny to reach into his breast pocket and pull out a tattered bag and a small bound journal, he complied. Hans told him that what was inside the bag would be their family's salvation. He made Danny swear he would follow his dying wish, and with that he was gone. The light faded from his eyes as Danny sobbed helplessly, pleading with his brother not to leave him again. He screamed at their medic, Alexander, to save his brother, but they all knew a mortal wound when they saw it.

Finally, after what felt like an eternity, Danny's friends gently pulled him off his brother and led him to a small alcove and told him to stay there. Meanwhile, they buried Hans in a shallow grave and left it unmarked for fear of what the Nazis would do to the bodies of deserters.

With a numb brain and a heavy heart Danny pulled Fritz away from his brother's grave and ordered him to fuss. Fritz reluctantly left the gravesite with Danny and their comrades.

It was a long, quiet journey back for the alliance. No one knew what to say to comfort Danny and suspected he would prefer to suffer in silence.

# -28-

After a full day on the road, Danny's team arrived back at their camp. Reb's team had already arrived the day before. After sharing what had happened with Reb, Danny told her he needed to go home to tell his parents. Reb tried to console Danny and asked if he wanted company. Danny refused, knowing he had to do this on his own. So that night Danny and Fritz went home, arriving around 10 pm. His parents were used to his unexpected appearances and never once asked where he had been spending his days and nights for fear of the answer. However, that night they knew something had changed as soon as they saw Danny's tear stained face. And Danny was finally ready to tell them everything, or just about everything; there were things they didn't need to know.

Danny told them the story he had rehearsed on the way home…how he had found Hans shot and bleeding, and barely alive. Danny hailed him as a hero for deserting the Nazi concentration camp and for killing a great many Nazis on his aborted attempt to get home. Danny apprised his parents that Hans wanted to apologize for his bad choices and planned to beg their forgiveness, which was all true.

Danny explained how they had tried in vain to save him, but his injuries had been too grave. He had been shot by an SS officer and left for dead. Then he showed them the pouch Hans had pressed into his hand vowing that this would save them all. Together they opened it.

Inside were sparkling jewels, at least a dozen priceless gems, including Frau Schwartz's diamond brooch...it was unmistakable. Upon seeing it, everyone gasped and looked at each other for an explanation. Of course, none of them had any ideas. Where Hans had gotten them they would never know. Now though, thanks to Hans, Danny informed them they would be going to America...what else could they do but honor Hans' dying wish.

It was a long night of explaining to his parents most of what he had been doing. Nevertheless, once their shock and horror subsided, Danny saw something else in their eyes...was it actually pride?

Next, it was his mutter's turn to confess. "My Gott Danny! I've known for some time that you were fighting the Nazis, but if I had known the extent to which you were involved I would have tried to stop you." She turned to her husband and admitted that she had been suffering in silence, constantly worrying about Danny. She told Jacob she had been too afraid to tell him what their youngest son had been up to for fear it would hurt him too deeply.

Without waiting for Jacob's reaction, Emma turned back to Danny, "I've been feeling so guilty. I thought I had inadvertently pushed you down this path when I asked you long ago why you hadn't stopped Hans from leaving. I figured that you were fighting to relieve your own guilt from not stopping your big brother. I thought that you were trying to compensate for that by killing the bastards who had taken Hans away. "

She let Danny know that she had ached to stop him, to protect him, but she knew he needed to do what he had done.

Emma desperately wanted Danny to know how she had agonized over what to do because she loved him so deeply.

Danny was astonished, yet extremely pleased to hear what his mutter had to say. He had felt so ignored and unloved over the last year. The family he had known had disappeared seemingly overnight that August day Hans had left home. The family he had known, who had been warm and loving people who discussed their days over dinner every evening, had become a distant memory. He had no idea what was going on in his parents' minds because they had basically stopped talking.

Danny had never really stopped to consider what had driven him to join the rebel army. He remembered how helpless he had felt as well as uncontrollable anger and frustration. It seemed that fate had indeed played a role as well. Maybe he had been out to prove something to his mutter, who only seemed to have been concerned about losing her oldest son. "Wow, talk about miscommunication," Danny thought chagrined. In the end though, Danny was not at all sorry for his choices. He was actually very proud of them.

As they continued to discuss all that had transpired and how they would get to America, into the wee hours of the morning, a sudden awful thought sprang to Danny's mind. He stood up suddenly and in no uncertain terms told his parents that they could leave if they wanted, but there was no way he was leaving without his dog. Fritz had saved his life on countless occasions and he would die before leaving him behind.

When his papa actually laughed, Danny had no idea what to make of that. Was he really laughing at Danny's demand, after everything he had been through? After all, he hardly knew his vater anymore. And when his vater stood up and said, "Don't be ridiculous!" Danny felt betrayed, and turned to leave, to head back to the only other family he had ever known.

Before he took even two steps, his papa grabbed him by the shoulder, spun him around, hugged him tightly, and said, "Danny, don't be ridiculous! There's absolutely no chance that we would even think of leaving Fritz behind!" Without him they knew Danny would never have survived. Fritz was a full-fledged member of their small family and Danny was filled with relief.

As the weeks of planning and bribery slowly passed, Danny wondered at the change that came over his parents. While devastated over the loss of their oldest son, perhaps they had been given the closure they needed; to know what had happened to Hans and to be able to be proud of his sacrifice. They slowly came back to being the people Danny had always respected and loved, instead of the shadows of themselves they had become. Thanks to Hans, they were all finally able to look to a future that they couldn't ever have imagined before.

## -29-

Danny went back to the Resistance many times in the ensuing weeks. On his final visit he spoke with Reb privately first, before he addressed the rest of the troops. They talked for hours about nothing in particular, just to stretch out their last moments together. Danny couldn't imagine a life without Reb in it, and when he told Reb about his plans and that she could come to America with them, she was overwhelmed with emotion. It was the only time he saw her cry. Tears, unbidden, ran down her face. She promised that one day she would, but for now, her place was here with her brothers and her comrades fighting against injustice. While very disappointed, Danny had suspected that would be Reb's decision, and he only admired and respected her more for it.

Danny had one more thing to ask Rebel before he spoke to the rest of the alliance. They spoke about Frau Z and all she had done for them, and how Danny wanted to do something for her. When he shared his idea Rebel readily agreed, saying they should have done it sooner.

When the time came to apprise the Resistance of his plans, Danny was very nervous. But instead of the opposition he expected, they all wished him well and a safe passage. They, of course, knew nothing about the stolen jewels or how Danny's family thought they would succeed. However, they all knew that Danny had served them well and he deserved a chance at a life that wasn't filled with bloodshed. And after losing his brother, it was time for Danny to start a new life.

Reb called for a celebration that night and spent every moment by Danny's side. Reb confessed that she loved Danny as a brother and told him she would miss him very much; however the way she held his hand and looked into his eyes belied that statement. Secretly, she knew her feelings for Danny were far deeper, and very different than what she felt for her brothers. Danny replied that he had never had a better friend and would miss her terribly; which was all true while disguising his true feelings for her. Reb gave Danny her parents' address so that he could write to her when he got to America and they could stay in touch. They parted with tears in their eyes and vowed that they would see each other again in the future; a brighter future where they could live normal lives.

At the last moment, Reb stuck out her hand to shake and said, "By the way, my name's Katherine."

Danny took her hand, but instead of shaking it, he discreetly pushed a small thick envelope into her palm and said, "It's a pleasure to meet you, Katherine. I look forward to the day you keep your promise and I hope this will help you do just that."

The members of the Resistance knew it was their destiny to carry on the war against those who had brought nothing but devastation to their beloved country, and Danny had given them the tools they needed to accomplish that. If one of their own could achieve a better life they were in full support of it. Danny realized that truer friends could not exist. Doing something they believed in together and risking their very lives in the process made them all more like brothers than friends.

## -30-

Danny had one last stop to make. He, Fritz and Gretchen walked together through the neighborhood that Danny had known all his life. While it was an old, dusty area with too many now vacant homes and businesses, he couldn't imagine living anywhere else. But in his heart, he knew he was making the right decision. It was his place now to look after his parents and Fritz and keep them all safe.

When Frau Z saw him at the door to her home, her face lit up with delight. She had come to love this young man and admire him for all he had accomplished, even with his disability. She was thrilled to see Fritz and meet Gretchen. It was how Danny had hoped it would be as Frau Z and Gretchen took to each other almost immediately. Gretchen was getting old now and it was time for her to be retired and live in comfort, while protecting her new mistress. After they had chatted over tea and Bavarian cream puffs, Danny told Frau Z that Gretchen was a gift for her. Knowing her love of dogs he wanted her to have a companion. She was over the moon with the idea and thanked Danny profusely. She was so happy she seemed to glow. When he told her that Rebel would be returning her car the next day, Frau Z grinned and said, as she smiled into Gretchen's intelligent eyes and ruffled her fur, "Oh, really, don't bother. I don't use it anyway. It is my gift back to the Resistance, and I know I got the better end of that deal!"

It broke Danny's heart to have to give her his other news. He told her what had happened on their last mission and how

Hans' had come through to save his family. Frau Z's eyes teared up as she empathized with Danny over the loss of his brother. She told him she knew he had never given up on Hans, and was glad he at least had gotten to see him one last time.

When Danny apprised her that his parents had been able to secure passage to America, she cried at the thought of never seeing Danny again. Danny embraced her and told her she could come with them. His parents had already agreed. Hans was right, Danny thought, it was great to have a lot of money for a change and be able to help your friends.

Frau Z hugged Danny to her once again and thanked him for this astonishing offer. But to Danny's amazement, she too declined. He had expected that Reb, rather Katherine, would feel the need to stay, but he had thought that Frau Z would accept their generous offer.

She explained that Danny had provided her with a new purpose in life, aiding his alliance, and that it gave her great satisfaction to do this. She didn't want to abandon them now. No amount of begging would change her mind, so Danny had to say good-bye to this wonderful woman, this surrogate mutter she had become, and it wasn't easy. Before he left he wrote down her address so that he could write to her from America. Leaving Gretchen with her did help alleviate the pain though. He knew they were a match made in heaven, and both would benefit greatly from each other. It made him feel warm inside to give back to Frau Z for all she had done for him.

On his way back home, Danny thought about how much he was going to miss Frau Z, but in a way it relieved him of some of the latent guilt he felt leaving the alliance behind. At least she would continue to look out for them and feed them. Through all the death and strife of the last year, Danny realized he had actually been very, very fortunate...he had made true friends and had helped out significantly in their moral, virtuous fight to end the genocide and help the innocent. Maybe what they had achieved might be considered by some to be insignificant in the overall scheme of things. Still, Danny at least felt he could hold his head high and was proud of what they had accomplished.

## -31-

It was an unusually mild day in January, 1940 when Danny and his family were at last on their way to America. Danny stood at the railing with Fritz at his feet and thought about Rebel, Frau Z, and Chaim. They had all been blessings in his life and he would miss each of them terribly. He held tight to the belief that Reb, rather Katherine, would keep her promise. He also prayed that it would all be over soon and that he would be able to come back and visit Frau Z and his comrades.

Finally his thoughts turned to Hans. He had read his brother's journal several times and each time he'd had to stop because his tears were staining the pages. His heart ached for all the pain Hans had suffered, especially with the loss of Chaim. He was even proud of Hans for how he had managed to escape that horrific place all on his own. He missed him with all of his heart, and would for the rest of his life.

Danny thought about whether he would have had the courage to do what Hans had done. Even if he had the conviction that joining the SS was the right thing to do, he didn't think he would have been able to go, to leave his home for Gott knew where and for Gott knew how long. He thought that what Hans had done took greater courage than what he himself had done. At least Danny had known what he was getting himself into and had been able to be prepared for it.

Maybe his brother's motives had been more pure than he had ever given him credit for. And even if they weren't, what did it really matter? His parents didn't need to know everything. It was best that they remembered their oldest son as a hero, as their savior; and Danny was happy to follow in his brother's giant shadow, as he always had before.

## Acknowledgements

For as long as I can remember I have always loved to write, and writing a book has been on my "bucket list" for quite some time. Now that I have retired from teaching, I could no longer procrastinate with the excuse that I don't have the time for such an endeavor.

In the past, while the desire to write a novel was there, I had no idea what I wanted my book to be about. My inspiration actually came to me two years ago in the form of a very elaborate dream - can you believe that?

However, I could not have done it without the help and encouragement of very dear family and friends. I owe a great debt of gratitude to the people who played a role in bringing this book to fruition.

First, and foremost, I want to thank my beloved son, David Betts, for his ideas, suggestions, his expertise in matters of weapons and warfare, and his help with editing. I owe a great deal of gratitude to my tech-savvy husband, John, for rescuing me on countless occasions when I had computer issues. I want to thank my dear friends, Kristen Green and Frannie Friedman for their unfailing support and advice. I need to thank Teresa Smith for her patient reviews of my manuscript and her expertise in editing and history. I must also thank Michele Papa for taking the time from her busy teacher's life to read my manuscript and offer me extremely helpful guidance. Finally, I need to thank my wonderful nephew, Brad Weiner, for his help with creating my website: brothersbysusan.com. Without his help, I'm sure I'd still be at it!

## Note to Reader

As Brothers was a work of historical fiction, I tried to stay true to the actual sequence of events that occurred during those horrific years of Hitler's reign of Germany. However, I have taken several creative licenses throughout my novel. For example, some dates aren't exactly accurate and I have included certain items in my story that hadn't actually existed at that point in time, such as plastic soda bottles and toilet paper (Really! Can you believe that?)

My goal was to teach about a dark time in history while making the reading enjoyable and entertaining at the same time. In addition, please note that smoking was not known to be a health hazard during that time, but I couldn't resist adding a touch of humor to lighten the mood after that violent scene in Chapter 21. I also wanted to show how Danny's feelings towards his missions had progressed.

Please forgive me!